THE LANCE
OF KANANA

A STORY OF ARABIA

BY

HARRY W. FRENCH
"ABD EL ARDAVAN"

j7888l

This special edition is published by arrangement with the publisher of the regular edition, Lothrop, Lee & Shepard Co.

CADMUS BOOKS
E. M. HALE AND COMPANY
CHICAGO

CONTENTS.

ENCIRCLED by the fiery, trackless sand,
  A fainting Arab halted at a well
Held in the hollow of the desert's hand.
    Empty! Hope vanished, and he gasped and
      fell.
At night the West Wind wafted o'er the land
  The welcome dew, a promise to foretell:
Hers this result, for which she bade him stand.

THE LANCE OF KANANA

I

THE COWARD OF THE BENI SADS

KANANA was an Arab—a Bedouin boy of many years ago, born upon the desert, of the seed of Ishmael, of the tribe of Beni Sad.

It seems well-nigh impossible that the Bedouin boy could have lived who was not accustomed to the use of the sword and lance, long before he reached the dignity of manhood.

The peculiar thing about Kanana was that he never held a lance in his hand but once; yet many a celebrated sheik and powerful chieftain of his day lies dead, buried, and forgotten long ago, while the name of Kanana is still a magic battle-

cry among the sons of Ishmael, and his
lance is one of the most precious relics of
Arabia.

The old mothers and the white-haired
veterans love to tell the story of the lance
of Kanana; their black eyes flash like coals
of fire when they say of it that it rescued
Arabia.

The Beni Sads were a powerful tribe
of roving Bedouins. Kanana was the
youngest son of the venerable chief; the
sheik who in the days of his strength was
known from the Euphrates to the sea as
the "Terror of the Desert."

By a custom older than the boyhood of
King David it fell to the lot of the youngest son to tend his father's sheep. The
occupation was not considered dignified.
It was not to Kanana's liking and it need
not have lasted long; for the Terror of the
Desert thought more of making warriors
than shepherds of his sons, but greatly to
his father's disgust Kanana refused to exchange his shepherd's staff for a warrior's

lance. It was not that he loved the staff, but that he objected to the lance.

The tribe called Kanana effeminate because he was thoughtful and quiet, where other boys were turbulent, and as he grew older and the boyish fancy became a decided conviction against the combats constantly going on between the different tribes, they even called him a coward and said that he did not dare to fight.

There is but one name more bitter than "coward" to the Arab. That name is "traitor," and after being called a coward almost all his life, the very last words which Kanana heard from the lips of his countrymen came in frantic yells, calling him a traitor.

To-day, however, it is always with throbbing hearts and flashing eyes that they repeat the story of the Lance of Kanana that rescued Arabia.

Until he was five years old, Kanana rolled about in the sand and sunshine, like the other children, with nothing on him but a twisted leather cord, tied round his waist.

Then, for five years, according to the custom of his people, he helped the women of his father's tent; shaking the goat-skin filled with cream till it turned into butter; watching the kedder upon the fire, drying the buttermilk to be ground into flour, and digging kemma, which grow like truffles, under the sand.

After he was ten, for three years he watched the sheep and goats and the she-camels. That was the regular course of education through which all Bedouin boys must pass.

When he reached the age at which Ishmael was sent away with Hagar by Abraham, he was supposed to drop all menial labor and take his place among men; making a position for himself according to the fighting qualities which he possessed.

Kanana's fighting qualities, however, were only exhibited in the warfare which now began between him and his father.

There were at that time very few occupations open to the Bedouin boy. The tribe was celebrated for its men of learning and boasted the most skillful physicians in all Arabia; but they had all won their first laurels with the lance, and none of them wanted Kanana.

Three times his father came to him with the question: "Are you ready to be a man?" and three times Kanana replied, "My father, I can not lift a lance to take a life, unless it be for Allah and Arabia."

How he came by a notion so curious no Arab could tell. The lad well knew the old decree that the hand of the Ishmaelite should be against every man, and every man's hand against him. He knew that every Arab of the desert lived by a warfare that was simply murder and robbery. Was he not an Arab, and an Ishmaelite?

Alone, among the sheep and camels, he had thought out his own theory. Kanana said to himself, "I am taught that Allah created these animals and cares for them, and that I cannot please him if I allow them to suffer; it must be surely that men are more precious to Allah than animals. Why should we kill one another, even if we are Arabs and Ishmaelites?"

The menial tasks still allotted to Kanana grew more and more irksome. His punishment was far more keen than the tribe supposed; no one dreamed of the sharp cringe of pain with which he heard even the children call him a coward.

There were some faculties which Kanana possessed that made the warriors all envy him. He had a remarkable power over animals. No other Beni Sad could ride a camel or a horse so fast as Kanana. The most refractory creature would obey Kanana. Then, too, Kanana was foremost in the games and races. No other shepherd's eye was nearly so quick as Kanana's to detect an enemy approaching the flocks at night. No other young Bedouin, watching the ripening grain, could throw a stone from his sling so far and so accurately at the robber birds.

These accomplishments, however, only made his father the more angry that Kanana would not turn his gifts to some more profitable end.

Every year for three months—from planting to harvest-time—the Beni Sads encamped upon a river bank, on the outskirts of the Great Desert.

The encampment numbered nearly five hundred tents set in four rows as straight as an arrow flies.

These tents, of black goats'-hair cloth, were seven feet high in the center and five feet high on the sides. Some of them were twenty feet broad, and each was divided by a beautiful hanging white Damascus carpet. The men occupied one side, and the women and children the other. The favorite mare and the most valuable of the camels always slept by the tent, and the master's lance stood thrust into the ground at the entrance.

Far as the eye could reach, up and down the sluggish river, a field of ripening grain filled the narrow space between the yellow water and the silver-gray of the desert sand.

Here and there, through the grain-field, rose curious perches—platforms, constructed upon poles driven into the ground. Upon these platforms watchers were stationed when the grain began to head, and there they remained, night and day, till it was harvested, frightening the birds away.

Once a day the women brought them food, consisting of buttermilk, dried and ground and mixed with melted butter and dates; these same women renewed the supply of stones to throw at the birds.

The watchers were old men, women who were not needed in the tents, and little children; but all alone, this year, upon the most distant perch, sat Kanana.

There was not one of the tribe but felt that he richly deserved this disgrace; and Kanana could see no way to earn their respect, no way to prove himself a brave fellow. He was glad that they had given him the most distant perch, for there he could bear his hard lot, away from jests and jeers.

The women who brought the food stopped for a long time at some of the perches, reporting all the news, but they never troubled themselves to relieve Kanana's solitude. The perches were too far apart for conversation. Kanana had always time enough to think, and as the grain grew yellow this year, he came to two positive conclusions. He firmly resolved that before the reapers entered that field he would do something to convince his people that he was not a coward; failing that, he would hang his head in shame, acknowledge that they were right, and fly forever from their taunts.

II

THE OLD SHEIK'S PROMISE

THE sun was beating fiercely down upon Kanana's perch, but he had not noticed it. The stones piled beside him for his sling were almost hot enough to burn his hand, but he did not realize it, for he had not touched them for a long time. The wooden dish of paste and dates stood in the shadow of the perch. He had not tasted them.

The pile of stones grew hotter and hotter. The hungry birds ate and quarreled and ate with no one to disturb them. The Bedouin boy sat cross-legged on his perch, heedless of everything, twisting and untwisting the leather cords of his sling, struggling to look into the mists that covered up his destiny.

"Hi, there! you slothful son of a brave

father! Look at the birds about you!
Are you dead, or only sleeping?" sounded
the distant but shrill and painfully distinct
voice of an old woman who, with two children much younger than Kanana, occupied
the next perch.

Kanana roused himself and sent the
stones flying from his sling till there was
not a bird in sight.   Then he sank into deep
thought once more; with his head resting
upon his hands he became oblivious to
everything.

Suddenly he was roused by the sound of
horses' hoofs upon the sandy soil, a sharp
rustling in the drying grain. He looked
up, as thoroughly startled as though he
had been sleeping, to see approaching him
the one person than whom he would rather
that any or all of the tribe of Beni Sad
should find him negligent at his post of
duty.

It was his father.

"Oh, Kanana! oh, Kanana!" cried the
old man, angrily. "Thou son of my old

age, why didst thou come into the world to curse me? When thou shakest the cream, the butter is spoiled. When thou tendest the sheep, they are stolen! When thou watchest the grain, it is eaten before thy face! What shall a father do with a son who will neither lift his hand among men nor bear a part with women? And now, when all the miseries of life have taken hold upon me and the floods cover me, thou sittest at thine ease to mock me!"

Kanana sprang down from his perch. Kneeling, he touched his forehead to the ground.

"My father, slay me and I will take it as a mercy from thy hand. Or, as I am fit for nothing here, bid me go, and among strangers I will beg. But thou shalt not, my father, speak of me as ungrateful, unfilial. I know of no flood of sorrow that has come down upon thee."

"Thou knowest not what they all know?" exclaimed the old man fiercely.

"I know of nothing, my father. Since

I came into the field, three weeks ago, no one has spoken to me but to chide me.''

"Then know now," replied the sheik reproachfully, "that of thy two brave brothers who went with the last caravan, one has returned, wounded and helpless, and the other, for an old cause of blood between our tribes, has been made a prisoner by Raschid Airikat. The whole caravan, with the white camel at its head, Raschid has taken, and he has turned with it toward Damascus.''

"Thy part of the caravan was very small, my father," said Kanana. "Only four of the camels were thine, and but for the white camel they were all very old. Their burdens, too, saving my brothers, were only honey and clay-dust, of little value.''

This was the simple truth, and evinced at least a very practical side to Kanana's mind; but it was not the kind of sympathy which the sheik desired, and his anger burst out afresh against Kanana.

"Ay, thou tender of flocks, and sleeper!" he cried. "Wouldst thou teach me the value of camels and merchandise to comfort me? And hast thou fixed the price of ransom which Airikat will demand, or slay thy brother? And hast thou reckoned up the value of the white camel which could not be bought for gold, as it brought to thy father and thy father's father all their abundance of good? Answer me, if thou art so wise. Oh, that I had a son remaining who could lift a lance against this Airikat as bravely as he hurls his empty words at an old father!"

"My father," said Kanana earnestly, "give me a horse, a sack of grain, a skin of water, and I will follow after Raschid Airikat. I will not slay him, but, by the help of Allah, I will bring back to thee thy white camel with my brother seated upon his back."

The old sheik made a gesture of derision: "Thou wisp of flax before a fire! Thou reed before a whirlwind! Get thee back

to thy perch and thy birds, and see if thou
canst keep awake till sundown. Harvesting will begin with the daylight to-morrow. See that thou workest then.''

Kanana rose to his feet. Looking
calmly into the old sheik's angry face, he
replied:

"My father, I will watch the birds till
sundown. Then let others do the reaping.
Kanana, whom thou scornest, will be far
away upon the desert, to seek and find his
brother.''

"Did I not say I would not trust a horse
to thee?" exclaimed the old man, looking
at him in astonishment.

"These feet of mine can do my bidding
well enough," replied Kanana. "And by
the beard of the Prophet they shall do it
till they have returned to thee thy son and
thy white camel. I would do something,
oh, my father, that I, too, might have thy
blessing and not thy curse. It is the voice
of Allah bids me go. Now say to me that
if I bring them back then thou wilt bless

me, too, ay, even though still I will not lift
a lance, unless it be for Allah and Arabia.''

The aged warrior looked down in a sort
of scornful pity upon his boy, standing
among the stalks of grain; half in jest,
half in charity, he muttered, ''Yes, *then* I
will bless thee,'' and rode away.

The harvesting began, as the old sheik
had said, with the next daylight, but Kanana was not among the reapers.

Few so much as missed him, even, and
those who did, supposed that he had hidden
himself to avoid their jests.

Only the sullen sheik, bowed under his
affliction, thought often of Kanana as he
rode up and down the line. He remem-
bered his looks, his words. He wondered
if he could have been mistaken in the boy.
He wished he had given him the horse and
that he had blessed him before he went
away.

III

AT THE FOOT OF MOUNT HOR

THE moment the sun sank into the billows of sand Kanana had left his perch.

From the loaded stalks about him he gathered a goat's-hair sack of grain and fastened it upon his back. There was no one to whom he need say farewell, and, armed only with his shepherd's staff, he started away upon the desert, setting his course to the north and west.

Before he had gone far he passed a lad of about his own age who had come from the encampment to hunt for desert-rats. Had Kanana seen him he would have made a wide détour, but the boy lay so still upon the sand that the first Kanana knew of his presence was when a low sarcastic voice uttered his name.

27

"Kanana!" it exclaimed. "Thou here! Dost thou not fear that some rat may bite thee? Whither darest thou to go, thus, all alone, and after dark, upon the sand?"

Fire flashed from Kanana's eyes. His hand clutched his shepherd's staff and involuntarily he lifted it; but the better counsel of his curious notions checked the blow. It was so dark that the boy upon the sand did not notice the effect of his taunts and knew nothing of his narrow escape. He only heard the quiet voice of Kanana as presently it meekly replied to his question:

"I go to Mount Hor."

It was an answer so absurd that the boy gave it no second thought and by the time that the foosteps of Kanana had died away the rat-hunter had as utterly forgotten him as though he had never existed.

To Mount Hor?

Kanana had only the most imperfect information to guide him. He knew that the Beni Sad caravan had been for some days upon the road southward, to Mecca, when it was captured by Raschid Airikat and turned at an angle, northward, toward Damascus.

Seen from a great distance, over the sea of sand, the solitary peak of old Mount Hor, where Aaron, the great high priest of Israel, was buried, forms a startling beacon. By day or night, it rises clear and sharp against the sky, guiding the caravans northward, from Arabia to Jerusalem and Damascus, and southward from Syria to Medina and Mecca; while the fertile oasis about it is the universal resting-place.

Kanana was not at all sure that the caravan would not have passed Mount Hor long before he could reach it; but if so, it must in time return that way, and, in any case, of all Arabia Mount Hor was the one spot where he could be sure to gather further information from passing caravans.

He knew his path upon that shifting sand as well as an Indian knew his way through the trackless forests of New England. With the sun and stars above him, any

Arab would have scorned the idea of being
lost in Arabia, and through the long night
with strong and steady strides Kanana
pressed onward toward Mount Hor.

As the harvest moon rose above the desert, behind him, the Bedouin boy was softly
chanting from the second *sura* of Al Koran:

> "God, there is no God but him;
> The Living!   The Eternal.
> Slumber doth not overtake him,
> Neither Sleep.
> And upholding all things,
> To him is no burden.
> He is the Lofty and the Great."

His long, black shadow fell over the sil-
ver sand, and, watching it, he chanted the
Koran again:

"God is God.   Whatever of good betideth thee
cometh from him.
"Whatever of evil is thine own doing."

Suddenly a speck appeared upon the distant horizon.   None but the keen eye of a
shepherd would have seen it, in the night,

but Kanana watched it as it quivered and wavered, disappearing as it sank into a valley in the rolling sand, appearing again, like a dory on the ocean, each time a little nearer than before.

Kanana noted the direction the speck was taking, and he made a wide path for it; he crouched among the sand-shrubs when it came too near.

First a small party of horsemen passed him, the advance guard of a moving tribe. Then came the main body of men upon camels and horses; but the only sounds were made by the feet of the animals and the clanking of the weapons. The she-camels with their young followed; then the sheep and goats driven by a few men on foot; next, the camels laden with the tents and furniture; last of all the women and children of the tribe accompanied by another armed escort.

From all that company there was not a sound but of the sand and the trappings. There was nothing but shadows, swinging, swaying shadows, moving like phantoms over the white sand, as the trailing train went gliding on, in that mysterious land of shadows and silhouettes.

There was nothing in it that was weird to Kanana, however. He hid himself simply as a precaution. He had often been a part of such a caravan, and he knew from experience, that if a solitary Arab were found upon the desert, he would very quickly be forced to help drive the sheep and goats, and kept at it until he could make his escape. Any Arab boy would have hidden himself.

Long before Kanana's next halt the sun was pouring down his furious heat. To his great good fortune he came upon a bowlder rising out of the sand; there he quickly made a place for himself where the sun could not reach him and lying down slept until night.

Only one who has walked upon a desert, hour after hour, parched with thirst and utterly exhausted in the fierce glare and

heat can properly appreciate the Bible pic-
ture of "the shadow of a great rock in a
weary land."

Had he not found this rock Kanana
would simply have dug a hole in the sand
and forced himself into it.

Here and there as he pressed on, Kanana
saw grim skeletons of men and animals as
they lay whitening among the sand-shrubs,
but he paid them little attention. Before
the sun had set, upon the second day, he
beheld the distant summit of Mount Hor
cutting sharply into the blue sky.

The sight renewed his strength. Hour
after hour he pressed onward, with his
eyes fixed upon the tomb of Aaron, a white
monument upon the summit of the moun-
tain, flashing like snow as the moon rose
in the clear, blue-black sky.

Kanana did not pause again until he fell
upon his knees beside the stream which
rises in a spring upon Mount Hor, to die in
the sand, not far from its base. He
plunged into the water; then, dressing him-

self again, he lay down upon the bank to
sleep. He awoke with the first gray light-
ing in the east, when the air of a desert is
almost cold enough to freeze.

He had now nothing more to do till he
could obtain some information from passing caravans. It would soon be sunrise,
the hour for morning prayer, and, to warm
himself while he waited, he walked along
the banks of the stream. They were blue
as the very sky, with masses of forget-me-
nots.

Suddenly Kanana paused. He started
back. His eyes dilated, and his hand trembled till the shepherd's staff fell, unheeded,
to the ground. The next moment he
dropped to the ground to examine the place
more carefully.

What was it? Only some marks upon
the grass where a caravan had camped.
The herbage was matted here and there
where the camels lay, and cropped short in
little circles about each spot where they
had eaten it as far as they could reach.

Caravans were continually resting for the day under the shadow of Mount Hor. There was nothing remarkable in the fact that a caravan had camped there, and had gone. They always move at night; not so much because it is cooler as because a camel will not eat at night, no matter how hungry he may be, and must be given the daylight or he will deliberately starve.

A moment later Kanana was upon his feet again with a triumph in his eyes which clearly indicated his satisfaction.

The grass about the spot was unevenly cropped; there were straggling spears of green left standing in the center of each mouthful which the camel had taken. Upon one side the bees were clustering on the matted grass. A multitude of ants appeared upon the other side. The imprint left by the forefoot of the camel showed that it had been extended in front of him, instead of being bent at the knee and folded beneath him.

All this meant to the young Arab that

the camel was old, that it was lame in the
left knee, that it had lost a front tooth, that
is burden on one side was honey, on the
other the dust of river clay, to be used in
the manufacture of stucco.

Had one of his father's camels stood before him Kanana could not have been more
sure.   Nothing more was needed to assure
him that Raschid Airikat, with the stolen
camels, had left Mount Hor the night before, upon the trail leading southward into
Arabia.

His eyes flashed with excitement. "My
brother and the white camel are not ten
hours from here, and they are on the road
to Mecca or Medina," he exclaimed as his
fingers tightened about the staff.

His white teeth glistened in a smile, as
he added, "They are mine, or I am a coward!"

He stood there, motionless, for a moment, his dark eyes instinctively turning
southward. The magnitude of his task lay
vividly before him. He recalled his fa-

ther's words: "Thou wisp of flax before a fire! Thou reed before a whirlwind!" They served to strengthen him.

The first step which lay before him was enough to test the courage of a brave man, and yet it was only a step toward a grand destiny.

Suddenly starting from his revery, Kanana exclaimed:

"I will do it! or I will consent to be known forever as the coward of the Beni Sads!" and turning he ran up the rocky sides of old Mount Hor, toward the white tomb of Aaron, whence he knew he could see far away over the great ocean of sand.

It might be there would yet appear a speck upon the distant horizon, to guide him toward the retreating caravan.

IV

THE PROMISE

UP the steep sides of Mount Hor, Kanana climbed, without waiting to look for a path. He saw nothing, heard nothing. He was all eagerness to reach the summit, in the faint hope that it might not be too late to see the departing caravan of Raschid Airikat.

Unless a camel is fresh, unusually large and strong, or constantly urged, it rarely makes more than two miles an hour. It was not over ten hours since the robber sheik had left the oasis, and some of the camels were very old and exhausted. It was a foolish hope, no doubt, and yet Kanana hoped that anything so large as a great caravan might still be distinguishable.

Up, up, up he climbed—as fast as hands

and feet could carry him. He no longer felt the cool air of early morning. He no longer looked about him to see the new sights of a strange oasis.

He did not even pause to look away over the desert as he climbed. The highest point was none too high. He did not care how far he could see until he had gained the white tomb of Aaron, upon the very crest.

Had he not been too thoroughly occupied with what was above him to notice what transpired about him and down below, he would have seen five Arab horsemen reach the stream by which he slept, almost as he began to climb.

They were Mohammedan soldiers, thoroughly armed for war, and had evidently come from the northern borders of Arabia, where the victorious Mussulmans were triumphantly planting the banner of Islam.

They had been riding hard, and both men and horses were exhausted. They hurried to the water. The men hastily ate some food which they carried, and tethered their horses in Arab fashion, by a chain, one end of which is fastened about the forefoot of the animal and the other end about the master, to prevent their being stolen while the master sleeps.

The moment this was accomplished, the five men rolled themselves in their mantles, covering their faces, as well as their bodies, and lay down upon the grass to sleep.

They were skilled in the art of making long journeys in the shortest possible time, and were evidently upon important business; for an Arab is never in haste unless his mission is very important.

Before Kanana reached the temple the men were soundly sleeping, and the horses, lying down to rest themselves, were still eating the grass about them, as a camel eats.

Panting for breath, and trembling in his eager haste, Kanana reached the tomb of Aaron: an open porch, with white pillars supporting a roof of white, like a crown of eternal snow upon the summit of Mount Hor.

Between the snowy pillars Kanana paused. One quick glance at the sky gave him the points of the compass, and shading his eyes from the glowing east, he looked anxiously to the south and west.

Sand, sand, sand, in billows like great waves of an ocean, lay about him in every direction. Far away there were low hills, and a semblance of green which, to his practiced eye, meant a grove of date palms upon the banks of a stream. But nowhere, search as he would, was there the faintest speck to indicate the caravan.

He was still anxiously scanning those distant hills when the first rays of the rising sun shot from the eastern horizon, flashing a halo of glory upon the snow-white crown of old Mount Hor, before they touched the green oasis lying about its base.

Never, in all the ages, had the sun come

up out of the Arabian desert to see such a
tableau as his first bright beams illumined
Aaron's tomb.

All absorbed in his eager search, Kanana
stood upon the very edge of the white
porch. One hand was extended, grasping
his shepherd's staff, the other was lifted to
shade his eyes.

In his eagerness to reach forward, one
foot was far before the other, and the knee
was bent, as though he were ready to leap
down the steep declivity before him.

His turban, a large square piece of cloth,
was bound about his head with a camel's-
hair cord; one corner was thrown back
over his forehead, and a corner fell
over each shoulder, like a cloak. His coat
was sheepskins stitched together. Sum-
mer and winter, rain and sunshine, the
Bedouin shepherd wears that sheepskin
coat, as the best protection against both
sun and frost.

His bare feet rested firmly upon the
white platform, and the arm that held the

shepherd's staff was knotted with muscles which a strong man might have envied him.

His beardless face was dark, but not so dark as to hide the eager flush which heightened the color in his cheeks, and his chest rose and fell in deep, quick motions from his rapid climb.

His lips were parted. His dark eyes flashed, while the hand which shaded them stood out from his forehead as though trying to carry the sight a little farther, that it might pierce the defiles of those distant hills and the shadows of the date palm groves.

The sun rose higher, and its full light fell across the young Ishmaelite. It was the signal for the morning call to prayer, and from the minaret of every mosque in the realm of Islam was sounding *La Illaha il Allah Mahamoud rousol il Allah*. Kanana did not need to hear the call, however. He instantly forgot his mission, and, a humble and devout Mohammedan, laid aside his staff and reverently faced toward Mecca to repeat his morning prayer.

Standing erect, with his open hands beside his head, the palms turned forward, he solemnly began the *Nummee Allah voulhamda*. With his hands crossed upon his breast he continued. Then he placed his hands upon his knees, then sat upon the floor. Then with his open hands upon the floor he touched his forehead to the platform as he repeated the closing words of the prayer.

In this position he remained for some time, whispering a petition of his own for strength and courage to carry out the task which he had undertaken.

There was something so solemn and impressive in the death-like stillness of the early morning, upon that solitary peak, that it almost seemed to Kanana that, if he listened, he should hear the voice of Allah, answering his prayer.

Suddenly the silence was broken by a sharp cry, and another and another in quick succession mingled with savage yells.

It was not the voice of Allah, for which he had been waiting, and Kanana sprang to his feet and looked anxiously about him.

The mountains of Arabia are not high. Among real mountains, Mount Hor would be but a rocky hill. Looking down, for the first time, Kanana saw the stream below him, in its border of blue forget-me-nots, and could clearly distinguish the five soldiers who had so quickly fallen asleep upon its banks.

It was a fearful sight which met his eyes. The five men were still lying there, but they were no longer sleeping. They were dead or dying; slain by three Bedouin robbers, who had crept upon them for the valuable prize of their horses, and who did not dare attempt to steal the animals while the masters were alive.

It was almost the first time that Kanana's eyes had rested upon a scene of blood, common as such scenes are among

his countrymen, and he stood in the porch
benumbed with horror, while the robbers
tore from the bodies about them such garments as pleased them; then took their
weapons, mounted three of the horses, and
leading two rode quickly away to the north.

There was no assistance which Kanana
could render the unfortunate men. The
caravan was already a night's march ahead
of him and every moment that he lost must
be redeemed by hurrying so much the
faster under the burning sun, over the
scorching sand, when, at the best, it was
doubtful if flesh and blood could stand what
must be required of it.

With a shudder he turned from the terrible scene and began to descend the moun-
tain. Soon he was upon the banks of the
stream and passing close to the spot where
the five bodies were lying. He would not
run, but he hurried on, with his eyes fixed
upon the ground before him.

A faint sound caught his ear. He
started, clutched his staff, and turned

sharply about, thinking that the robbers had seen him and returned. It was only one of the unfortunate soldiers who had been left for dead. He had raised himself upon his elbow, and was trying to attract Kanana's attention.

"Water! water! In the name of Allah, give me water!" he gasped, and fell back unconscious.

For a moment Kanana was tempted to hurry on. He did not want to go there, any more than he wanted to delay his journey; but something whispered to him of the promises of the Koran to those who show mercy to the suffering; that Allah would reward even a cup of water given to the thirsty.

It required no little courage of the Bedouin boy, all alone under Mount Hor, but he resolutely turned back, filled with water the wooden cup which a shepherd always carries at his girdle, and poured it down the parched throat of the almost insensible man.

"Bless God for water!" he gasped,
"More! give me more!"

Kanana ran to the brook and filled the
cup again, but the poor man shook his head.
It was too late. He was dying.

Suddenly he roused himself. He made
a desperate struggle to call back his failing
senses, and, for a moment, threw off the
hand of Death.

He had almost given up, forgetting
something of great importance. Steady-
ing himself upon his elbow, he looked into
Kanana's face and said:

"You are a beardless youth, but you
are an Arab. Listen to me. The mighty
Prince Constantine, son of the Emperor
Heraclius, is soon to leave Constantinople,
at the head of a vast army of Turks and
Greeks and Romans, like the leaves of the
forest and the sand of the desert. He is
coming to sweep the Arab from the face of
the earth and the light of the sun. We
were bearing a letter to the Caliph Omar,
who is now at Mecca, telling him of the

danger and asking help. If the letter does not reach him Arabia is lost and the Faithful are destroyed. Would you see that happen?''

Too frightened to speak and hardly comprehending the situation, Kanana simply shook his head.

The man made another effort to overcome the stupor that had almost mastered him. He succeeded in taking from his clothing a letter, sealed with the great seal, and gasped:

''In the name of Allah, will you fly with this to the great caliph?''

Hardly realizing what he said, Kanana solemnly repeated: ''In the name of Allah, I will.''

He took the letter and was hiding it in his bosom when the soldier grasped the cup of water, drank ravenously, and, with the last swallow, let the cup fall from lifeless fingers.

Minute after minute passed, but Kanana did not move a muscle. His hand still touched the letter which he had placed in his bosom. His eyes still rested upon the lips that would never speak again.

His sacred promise had been pledged to fly with that letter to the great caliph at Mecca. It had been made in the name of Allah. It had been given to the man now lying dead before him. There was no power that could retract it. It must be performed, and until it was performed no other consideration could retard his steps or occupy his thoughts.

His lips parted and he muttered, angrily: "Is this my reward for having given a cup of water to the thirsty?" Then it suddenly occurred to him that the caravan which he longed most of all to follow was also upon its way southward, and that, for the present at least, for either mission the direction was the same, and the demand for haste was great.

He caught his staff from the ground and set his face toward Mecca, pondering upon the dying statement of the soldier till word

for word it was fastened in his memory,
and the thought that his mission was for
Allah and Arabia urged him on.

It was an easy task to follow the trail
of the caravan. The Bedouin would be a
disgrace to the desert who could not recognize in the sand the recent footprint of one
of his own tribe or of a camel with which
he was familiar, and who could not tell by
a footprint whether the man or camel who
made it carried a burden, often what that
burden was, always whether he was fresh
or exhausted, walking leisurely or hurrying.

So Kanana hurried on, daily reading
the news of the caravan before him as he
went, testing his strength to the utmost
before he rested, and starting again as soon
as he was able; over the sand and over the
hills, through groves and villages and over
sand again; always toward Mecca.

V

LED BY A WHITE CAMEL

IN the world-famous city of Mecca, two
men stood by the arch that leads to the
immortal Caaba.

They were engaged in an earnest conversation, heedless of everything about
them, when the distant cry of a camel driver
sounded on the still air.

Both of the men started and looked at
each other in surprise. One of them said:
"A caravan at the gate at this time of
day!" for it was several hours past mid-
day and a caravan, in the ordinary course
of things, reaches a city gate during the
night or very early in the morning.

Arabia was seeing troubled times, and
every one was on the alert for anything out
of the accepted rule.

The camel-driver's cry was repeated. The first speaker remarked:

"They have left the burdened camels at the Moabede gate and are entering the city."

With an anxious look upon his face the elder of the two replied, "Either they have been hard pressed by an enemy or it is important news which brings them over the desert in such haste, in this insufferable heat."

The two men were evidently of great importance in the holy city. They were surrounded by powerful black slaves, who had all that they could do to keep the passers-by from pressing too close upon the elder man, in a desire to touch the hem of his garment. Many, in passing, knelt and touched their foreheads to the ground. Thus they waited the coming caravan.

The first camel of an important caravan is led by a man who walks before it, through the narrow streets of a city, and his cry is to warn the crowd to clear the way;

there being no sidewalks, and, indeed, but very little street.

"There it comes," said the younger of the two, as the long line of drowsy camels appeared, swinging, swinging, swinging along the narrow street.

"Led by a white camel," added the elder, and they both looked down the street.

The lead-camel was larger than the rest —much larger, and very much lighter colored; a sort of dingy white, like a sheep before shearing. The chief of the caravan sat upon his back, as unmindful of everything as though he were still upon the trackless sand.

It is not impossible that the sheik was really sleeping, and unconsciously grasping his ugly lance, while his Damascus blade hung ready by his side.

He roused in a moment, however, for with many a grunt and groan the great, ungainly, and yet very stately, ships of the desert came slowly and drowsily to anchor in the court before the Caaba.

"*Haji,*" a naked little urchin muttered, looking up from his play; but he should have known better. *Haji* means pilgrims, and these were no pilgrims.

There are seasons when this city is one mass of humanity. Haji by hundreds and thousands throng the narrow streets, but these are Bedouins of the desert, bound upon some other mission than worshiping before the Caaba, kissing the Black Stone, or drinking the holy water of Zemzem.

The leader of the white camel gave a peculiar pull to the rope hanging over his shoulder, attached to the animal's bridle, and uttered a short, sharp word of command.

Slowly, very slowly, the dignified, dingy creature, towering high above him, acknowledged the receipt of the order, but he gave no evidence that he was making any arrangements to obey.

His response was simply a deliberate grunt and a weird and melancholy wail that came gurgling out of his long, twisting throat. He would not have hurried himself one atom, even for the sheik upon his back.

A white camel is to the Arab what a white buffalo is to the Indian and a white elephant to the Ceylonese, and he fully appreciates his importance.

He deliberately turned his woolly head quite about till his great brown eyes, with the drooping lids almost closed over them, could most conveniently look back along the line of lank, inferior camels, and gaunt and weather-beaten dromedaries, which had patiently followed him, day after day, to the temple court of immortal Mecca.

He was so long about it that the leader repeated the command and very slowly the camel brought his head back again, till his languid eyes looked drowsily down, in a sort of scornful charity, upon the insignificant mortal at the other end of his halter.

He had stood in the court of Mecca long before that man was born and would doubtless guide caravans to the same spot long after he was buried and forgotten.

"You may be in haste, but I am not," he seemed to say, and dreamily turned his eyes toward the black-curtained Caaba, as if to see how it had fared since his last visit.

That Caaba, the Holy of Holies of the Mussulman, is the most revered and possibly the most venerable of all the sacred buildings on the earth; but the gentle, wistful eyes of the white camel were more practically drawn toward two or three date-palm-trees then growing beside it. When he had satisfied himself that the only green thing in sight was quite beyond his reach, he deliberately lowered his head, changed his position a little, and with another grunt and another melancholy wail sank upon his knees, then upon his haunches. With a deep sigh he lifted his head again still high above the head of his driver, and his drowsy eyes seemed saying to him:

"Poor man! I kept you waiting, didn't I?"

Then he quickly turned his head to the opposite side, deliberately poking his nose into the passing throng, till, with a grunt of recognition, it touched the garment of one who was hurrying on among the crowd.

It was evidently a Bedouin, but the wings of his turban were drawn together in front, so that no one could see his face. He responded to the greeting of the white camel, however, by laying his hand upon the creature's nose as he passed. It was a motion which no one noticed, and a moment later he was out of sight.

He was following a boy who had led him directly to the arch, where the boy paused, pointed to the elder of the two men standing there, briefly observing:

"It is he."

The Bedouin paused for a moment, as if struggling to collect his thoughts, then hurrying forward was the next to prostrate himself before the venerable man. As he rose he handed him a package, simply observing:

"A message to the Caliph Omar."

The great caliph quickly broke the seal and read; then, turning to the bearer, asked sharply, "And who art thou?"

"I am Kanana, son of the sheik of the Beni Sads," replied the Bedouin boy, letting the wings of his turban fall apart that Omar might see his face.

"A beardless youth!" exclaimed the caliph. "And dost thou know aught of the import of this letter?"

Kanana repeated the dying words of the Arab soldier, which had so often escaped his lips as he urged his weary feet toward Mecca.

"'Tis even so," replied the caliph. "And how came living man to trust a boy like you to come alone, through the streets of Mecca, with such an errand?"

"I came alone with the letter from the oasis at Mount Hor," replied Kanana, straightening himself up, with very pardonable pride, before the astonished eyes of the great caliph.

Then he related, briefly, how the letter came into his keeping, and the dangers and escapes of the three long weeks during which he carried it in his bosom; each rising and setting sun finding it a little nearer to its destination.

"Thou art a brave youth," said the caliph, "a worthy son of the Terror of the Desert. Would to Allah that every Arab had thy heart, and Heraclius himself, with all the world behind him, could not move the Faithful from their desert sands. And they shall not be moved! No! By the beard of the Prophet, they shall not be moved. Hear me, my son; I will see more of thee. This is no place for conversation, where the wind bloweth into what ears it listeth. One of my slaves shall conduct you to my house. There I will meet you presently. Go, and Allah go with you."

Indicating the slave who should take Kanana in charge, the Caliph Omar turned abruptly away and showed the letter to the man with whom he had been conversing.

VI

KANANA AND THE CALIPH

GUIDED by the black slave, Kanana passed out again under the arch, and walked the streets of Mecca, caring less and thinking less concerning what transpired about him than any one, before or since, who for the first time stood in the holy city.

He found the narrow streets densely crowded. Soldiers and merchants, Bedouins and city Arabs mingled with an array of every tribe Arabia could furnish. There were venders of all things pertaining to the necessities or luxuries of life; water-carriers with goatskins on their shoulders; fruit-criers with wooden trays upon their heads; donkeys laden with cumbersome baskets, beneath which they were almost lost to sight; camels carrying packs of a thousand pounds weight upon their backs, as though they were bundles of feathers; everything hustling and jostling, men and boys shouting and pushing for the right of way.

They all turned out as best they could, however, for the savage black slave of the great caliph, and by keeping close behind him Kanana always found an open space where he could walk without fighting for room.

It was almost the first experience of the Bedouin boy in real city life, and the very first time that his bare feet had ever touched the beaten sand of the unpaved streets of his most sacred Mecca.

He turned from the arch, however, without once glancing at the black-curtained Caaba, the Beitullah, or House of God, toward which three times a day he had turned his face in reverent devotion, ever since he had learned to pray.

He followed the black slave onward through the streets, without so much as looking at the walls of the houses that crowded close on either hand.

He had fulfilled his vow. The packet he had sacredly guarded through many a hardship and danger and narrow escape was safely delivered. Now he was free to carry on the work for which he left the perch and the birds in the grain-field of the Beni Sad.

Sometimes he thought of the black slave before him, and wondered if, after all, he was quite free. And the thought troubled him.

It seemed as though long years had passed since the day when his father met him with the news of Raschid Airikat's capture of his brother. He had suffered privations enough for a lifetime since then. More than once his life had hung by a slender thread. He could hardly imagine himself again sitting up on the perch, frightening the birds away, his life had so entirely changed; his determination to keep the vow he made his father had grown stronger every day; only he realized more the magnitude of the task he had undertaken; and he appreciated his father's words: "Thou wisp of straw before a fire! Thou reed before a whirlwind!" Still he gathered hope, because he was beginning to understand himself.

The dangers and hardships of one enterprise he had met and overcome, and under the very shadow of the Caaba, the great caliph of Mecca had called him brave.

Now he was eager for the next. There was no vital need of another interview with the caliph, and Kanana thought that if he could only escape from the black slave, by darting into a crowded alley, he could go at once about his own important business.

For the first time Kanana looked about him. At the moment there was no opportunity, and while he watched for one, the slave turned suddenly into a great gate, crossed a court paved with limestone, lifted a reed curtain, entered one of the most substantial stone structures of Mecca, and in-

dicated to Kanana the apartment in which
he was to wait for the caliph. It was too
late to escape. With all the patience and
dogged submission to destiny so strongly
developed in the Bedouin, Kanana sat down
upon a rug. There were luxurious otto-
mans about the room, and divans taken
from the palaces of Persian princes, but
the Bedouin boy preferred the desert seat.
Much as though he were still upon the
perch, he laid his staff beside him and
buried his face in his hands. The magnifi-
cence in this chamber of Omar's official resi-
dence only disturbed his thoughts.

He became so deeply buried in his plans
that he had entirely forgotten where he
was, when the rattle of the reed curtain
roused him and, starting from his dream,
he found the great caliph entering.

Reverently touching his forehead to the
floor, Kanana remained prostrate until the
caliph was seated. Then he rose and stood
leaning upon his staff while the old ruler
silently surveyed him. It seemed to Ka-

nana that his very heart was being searched
by those grave and piercing eyes.

Upon the shoulders of the Caliph Omar
rested the fate of Islam for future ages;
his word was law wherever Mohammed
was revered. He could have little time to
waste upon a shepherd boy; yet he sat for
a long while, silently looking at Kanana.
When he spoke, it was only to bid him repeat, at greater length, the story of how he
came by the letter and how he brought it
to Mecca.

"My son," he said, when Kanana had
finished, "thou hast done what many a
brave man would not have ventured to attempt. Ask what reward thou wilt of me."

"I would have the blessing of the Caliph
Omar," Kanana replied.

"That thou shall have, my son; and
camels, or sheep, or gold. Ask what thou
wilt."

"I have no use for anything. I ask thy
blessing, my father, and thy word to bid me
go."

"Thou art a strange lad," replied the caliph. "Thou art like, and yet unlike the Terror of the Desert. I command thee, my son, say what I can best do for thee."

"Give me thy blessing, then let me go, my father," repeated Kanana, kneeling. "More than that, if I took it, I should leave at thy gate."

Omar smiled gravely at the boy's obstinacy.

"If I can do nothing for thee, there is yet something which thou canst do for me. Kahled is the greatest general who fights for the Prophet. He will soon reach Bashra, with thirty thousand warriors. He will turn to enter Persia, but these letters must reach him, with my orders that he go again to Syria. Bashra is three weeks from here, and a company of soldiers will start to-night to carry the messages, while I send far and wide for the Faithful to join him. It would be well, my son, for thee to go with the soldiers, to give the story to Kahled by word of mouth."

"The way is hard. The sand is deep and dry between Mecca and Bashra," said Kanana. The caliph looked in some surprise upon the hardy Bedouin boy.

"Hardship should not be hard to thee; but thou shall be carried as one whom the caliph would honor."

"The way is dangerous. Robbers and hostile tribes are like the sand about Bashra," added Kanana, who had often heard of the countries along the eastern borders of Arabia.

Surprise became astonishment. The caliph exclaimed:

"Thou! son of the Terror of the Desert, speaking of danger?"

"My father, I spoke for thy soldiers," replied Kanana, quickly. "Before they reach the sands of Bashra they will be with the five who started with this letter. Dost thou believe that Kanana spoke in fear or cowardice? If so, give him the letters, and with thy blessing and the help of Allah, he will deliver them to thy Kahled, though every river run with fire, and the half of Arabia stand to prevent him!''

"Beardless youth!" cried the caliph. "I am too old for mockery."

"My father, without a beard I brought that letter here, and He who guarded me will guard me still."

"Wouldst thou dare to go without an escort?"

"I would rather have a sword I could not lift than have an escort," replied Kanana.

"By the beard of the Prophet, my son, there is both foolishness and wisdom in thy words. Thou shall take the messages by one route, and by another I will send the soldiers with copies. It may be that Allah guides thy tongue. When wilt thou start?"

"Now," replied Kanana.

"That was well spoken," said the caliph. "What camels and servants shall be provided?"

"My father," said Kanana, "as I came

a little way with the caravan which arrived to-day, I noted the white camel that took the lead. I never saw so great power of speed and endurance in a camel of the plain. The man who led him knew him well and was easily obeyed. I would have the two, none other, and the swiftest dromedary in Mecca, with grain for fourteen days."

The caliph shook his head: "It will be twenty days and more."

"My father, the burden must be light that the sand lie loose beneath their feet, and small, that it tempt no envious eye." Then, in the direct simplicity resulting from his lonely life, Kanana added, "If it is a three weeks' journey for others, in fourteen days thy messages shall be delivered."

The caliph summoned an officer, saying, "Go to the caravan at the Moabede Gate. Say that Omar requires the white camel and the man who leads it; none other. Bid Ebno'l Hassan prepare my black dromedary and food for the two for fourteen

days. Have everything at the gate, ready
to start, in half an hour." Then to a
slave, he added, "Give to the son of the
Terror of the Desert the best that the
house affords to eat and drink."

Without another word the caliph left the
room to prepare the messages. The slave
hurried to produce a sumptuous feast.
The officer left the house to execute the
orders of the man whose word was law.

Alone, Kanana sat down again upon the
mat and buried his face in his hands, as
though he were quietly preparing himself
to sleep.

Only a whisper escaped his lips. The
words were the same which he had angrily
spoken under the shadow of Mount Hor,
but the voice was very different: "This is
my great reward for giving a cup of water
to the thirsty. *La Illaha il Allah!*" The
slave placed the food beside him, but he
did not notice it. Not until the caliph entered again did he suddenly look up, ex-
claiming, "This shepherd's coat would

not be fitting the dignity of the white camel. I must have an *abbe* to cover it, and a mantle to cover my face, that Mecca may not see a beardless youth going upon a mission for the great caliph."

They were quickly provided. The camel and its driver were at the gate, with the black dromedary. All was ready, and with the mantle drawn over his beardless face, and the *abbe* covering his sheepskin coat, Kanana knelt and received the blessing of the Caliph Omar.

As he rose from his knees, the caliph handed him, first the letters, which Kanana placed in his bosom, and next a bag of gold which Kanana held in his hand for an instant; then, scornfully, he threw it upon the mat, remarking, "My father, I have already received a richer reward than all the gold of Mecca."

The caliph only smiled: "Let each one dance according to the music which he hears. My son, I see the future opening before thee. This is not thy last mission.

I read it in thy destiny that thou wilt succeed, and succeed again, until the name of Kanana be written among the greatest of those who have lifted the lance for Allah and Arabia. Go now, and God go with thee.''

VII

THERE was a group of several people standing about the caliph's gate as Kanana emerged. They were apparently waiting, in careless curiosity, to see the white camel start, and learn what they could of what was going on in official departments.

The information they received was very meager, yet it proved sufficient for more than one. They saw the white camel rise, with the veiled messenger of Omar upon its back. As the driver looked up to receive his first command their necks were bent in a way that betrayed their eagerness to hear. Only one word was spoken, however. It was "Tayf," the name of a city a short distance to the east of Mecca.

The camel-driver's cry sounded again through the streets, but the twilight shadows were gathering. There were few abroad, and the cries were not so loud or so often repeated as in the afternoon. When they ceased altogether, Kanana had turned his back upon Mecca forever.

The night wind blew cool and refreshing from the surrounding hills as the little caravan moved out upon the plain, but Kanana was ill at ease.

It was still as death in the valley. Far as the eye could penetrate the darkness they were all alone, except for five horsemen who left the gate of Mecca not long after the white camel, and were now riding slowly toward Tayf, a short distance behind it.

Ever and again Kanana looked back at them. The faint shadows, silently moving onward through the gloom, were always there; never nearer; never out of sight.

Leaning forward, he spoke in a low voice to the driver, "You walk as though you

were weary. The dromedary was brought
for you. Mount it, and follow me."

"Master," replied the driver, "the white
camel is obstinate. He will only move for
one whom he knows well."

"You speak to the wind," muttered Kanana. "Do as I bid thee. Hear my words.
Yonder black dromedary has the fleetest
foot in Mecca. He is the pride of the
Caliph Omar. Mount him, and if you can
overtake me while I drive the white camel,
you shall throw the dust of the desert in
the face of Raschid Airikat, and have the
white camel for your own."

The driver started back, and stood star-
ing at the veiled messenger of Omar. The
word, "Mount!" was sternly repeated.
Then he quickly obeyed, evidently bewil-
dered, but well satisfied that he would have
an easy task before him, from the moment
the white camel realized that a stranger
was in command.

Kanana spoke, and the camel started.

The dromedary moved forward close behind it without a word from the driver.
The horsemen had approached no nearer
while they waited, though Kanana had pur-
posely given them time enough to pass, had
they not halted when he halted. They
were still five silent shadows upon the distant sand.

"Faster," said Kanana, and the long
legs of the white camel swung out a little
farther over the sand and moved more rapidly, in response.

The dromedary immediately quickened
its pace without urging, and, a moment
later, from far in the distance, the night
wind brought the sound of horses' hoofs
through the silent valley. It was very
faint, but distinct enough to indicate that
the shadows behind them had broken into
a canter.

The camel-driver gave little heed to his
surroundings. He was too thoroughly
engrossed in the prospect of owning the

white camel to care who might be coming
or going in a way as safe as that from
Tayf to Mecca.

Kanana, however, who could walk
through the streets of the holy city without so much as knowing what the houses
were made of, would have heard the wings
of a night-moth passing him, or seen a
sand-bush move, a quarter of a mile away.

His life as a shepherd had, after all, not
been wasted.

"Faster," said Kanana, touching the
camel's neck with his shepherd's staff, and
without even the usual grunt of objection,
the animal obeyed. The sand began to fly
from his great feet as they rested upon it
for an instant, then left it far behind; the
Bedouin boy sat with eyes fixed on the path
before him, and his head bent so that he
could catch the faintest sounds coming from
behind. The mantle that had covered his
face fell loosely over his shoulder.

The dromedary lost a little ground for a
moment, but gathering himself together,

easily made it up.   The driver was too sure of the final result to urge him unduly at the start.   Soon enough the white camel would rebel of his own accord, and till then it was quite sufficient to keep pace with him.

The sound of horses' hoofs became sharper and more distinct, and Omar's messenger knew that the five shadows were being pressed to greater speed, and were drawing nearer.

"Faster!" said Kanana, and the white camel broke into a run, swinging in rapid motions from side to side, as two feet upon one side, then two on the other were thrown far in front of him and, in an instant, left as far behind.

Still the dromedary made light work of keeping close upon his track, evidently realizing what was expected of him; but the driver saw with dismay how quickly the camel responded to the word of his rider, how easily the man sat upon the swaying back—how carefully he selected the best path for the animal, and how skillfully he guided him so that he could make the best speed with the least exertion.

Many a night Kanana had run unsaddled camels about the pastures of the Beni Sads, guarding the sleeping sheep and goats, little dreaming for what he was being educated.

The sound of horses' hoofs grew fainter. They were losing ground, but now and then the listening ear caught the sharp cry of an Arab horseman urging his animal to greater speed.

"They are in earnest," muttered the Bedouin boy, "but they will not win the race."

"Faster!" said Kanana; the camel's head dropped till his neck lost its graceful curve, and the great white ship of the desert seemed almost flying over the billowy sand.

For a moment the dromedary dropped behind. The driver had to use the prod and force him to the very best that was in him, before he was able to regain the lost ground.

The sound of hoofs could no longer be heard, and Kanana was obliged to listen with the utmost care to catch the faintest echo of a distant voice.

"They are doing their best and are beaten, but we can do still better," he said to himself with a deep sigh of relief, as he watched the desert shrubs fly past them in fleeting shadows, scudding over the silver-gray sand.

The music of the sand, as it flew from the camel's feet and fell like hail upon the dry leaves of the desert shrubs, was a delightful melody, and hour after hour they held the rapid pace; over low hills and sandy plains; past the mud village and the well that marks the resting-place for caravans, a night's journey from Mecca, without a sign of halting; and on and on, the dromedary always just so far behind, always doing his best to come nearer.

If by urging he was brought a little closer

to the camel, the driver heard that low word, "Faster!" and in spite of him the camel gained again. Would he never stop?

The sounds from behind had long been lost when, far in advance, appeared the regular caravan from Tayf. They approached it like the wind. Only the mystic salaam of the desert was solemnly exchanged, then, in a moment, the trailing train as it crept westward was left, disappearing in the darkness behind them.

When it was out of sight the white camel suddenly changed its course, turning sharply to the north of east and striking directly over the desert, away from the hills and the beaten track to Tayf which he had been following.

The driver could not imagine that such a man as sat upon the white camel had lost his way. He silently followed till they passed a well that marked the second night's journey from Mecca toward Persia.

The driver and dromedary would very

willingly have stopped here; but the camel glided onward before them through the changing shadows of the night, as though it were some phantom, and not a thing of flesh and blood.

By dint of urging, the driver brought the dromedary near enough to call:

"Master, we are not upon the road to Tayf."

"No," said Kanana, but the camel still held his course.

Driven to desperation, as the eastern sky was brightening, the driver called again:

"Master, you will kill the camel!"

"Not in one night," said Kanana; "but if you value your own life, come on!"

Faster still and faster the white camel swept toward the glowing east, but the dromedary had done his best. He could not do better.

More and more he fell behind, and in spite of every effort of the driver, the pride of the caliph was beaten.

Fainter and fainter grew the outline of

the white camel against the morning sky,
ever swinging, swinging, swinging, over
the silver-gray sea, with a motion as regular and firm as though it had started but
an hour before.

As the red disc of the fiery sun rose out
of the desert, however, the driver saw the
camel pause, turn half about, till his huge
outline stood out in bold relief against the
sky, and then lie down.

Quickly Kanana dismounted. He caressed the camel for a moment, whispering, "We are two days and a half from
Mecca! Thou hast done better than I
hoped. Thou didst remember me yesterday in the temple court. To-night thou
hast cheerfully given every atom of thy
strength to help me. To-morrow we shall
be far apart. Allah alone knows for what
or for how long; but if we ever meet again
thou wilt remember me. Yes, thou wilt
greet thy Kanana."

The boy's dark eyes were bright with
tears as he gave the camel the best of the

food provided for him; then, with sand in
stead of water performing the morning ab-
lution, he faced toward Mecca.

When the dromedary and his rider
reached the spot, the veiled messenger of
Omar was solemnly repeating his morning
prayer.

VIII

ALL in vain the camel driver sought to obtain one glimpse beneath the mantle, to see the face of the caliph's messenger or to learn anything of their destination.

He prepared their very frugal breakfast without a fire, and, when it was eaten, in the humble, reproachful tone of one who felt himself unjustly suspected, he said:

"My master, why didst thou deceive me, saying we should go to Tayf? Didst thou think that I would not willingly and freely lead the white camel anywhere, to serve the great caliph?"

"There were other ears than yours to hear," replied Kanana.

"There were only beggars at the gate, my master. Dost thou believe I would be treacherous to a servant of Omar and the Prophet?''

"I believe that every child of Ishmael will serve himself," replied Kanana; "but that had nothing to do with what I said. Before we start to-night, I will lay out your path before you, to the very end. As for the beggars, where were your senses? For three days, in disguise, I journeyed with the caravan of Raschid Airikat, as it came to Mecca. I saw in him a treacherous man, and when he yielded to a command he must obey and gave me the white camel and his driver, I knew that he would take them back again by stealth and treachery, if he were able to. Have I no eyes, that I should spend three days with the caravan and then not recognize the servants of Airikat, though they were dressed as beggars and slunk away, with covered faces, into the shadows of the caliph's gate? They did not cover their feet, and by their feet I knew them, even when they deceived you, one of their own. To them I said,

'Go, tell your master that his white camel is on the way to Tayf.' "

"My master," said the driver, respectfully, "the sheik Airikat is as devout as he is treacherous and brave. He gave the sacred camel and thy servant willingly, at the command of Omar, for the service of Allah and Arabia. I do not think he would deal treacherously."

Kanana did not reply, for far away over the desert, to the east, there was a little speck of dark, like a faint shadow, upon the sand. He sat in silence watching it through the folds of his mantle, as it grew larger and larger, and a long caravan approached.

The camels were worn out from a long journey. Their heads hung down, and their feet dragged languidly over the sand. Their slow progress had belated them, and the sun would be several hours above the desert when they reached the oasis by the well, which the two had passed before daylight.

As they drew nearer it could easily be seen that the camels bore no burdens but necessary food, in sacks that were nearly empty, and that their riders were savage men from the eastern borders of Arabia.

"Master, do they see us?" muttered the driver.

"They have eyes," replied Kanana. And they had. A fresh dromedary and a white camel alone upon the desert, were a tempting prize.

They evidently determined to appropriate them; for, leaving the main body of the caravan standing in the path, twenty or more turned suddenly, and came directly toward them.

"Master, we must fly from them," whispered the driver.

"If they were behind us I would fly," replied Kanana, "for every step would be well taken; but my path lies yonder." He pointed directly toward the caravan. "And I would not turn from it though devils instead of men were in the way."

"It is the will of Allah. We are lost,"
muttered the camel-driver, and his arms
dropped sullenly upon his knees, in the
dogged resignation to fate so character-
istic of the Bedouin.

Kanana made no reply, but, repeating
from the Koran, " 'Whatever of good betideth thee cometh from Him,' " he rose
and walked slowly to where the white camel
was lying.

Upon the high saddle, which had not yet
been removed, hung the inevitable lance
and sword, placed there by the officer of
the caliph.

Leaning back against the saddle to await
the approach of the caravan, the Bedouin
boy threw his right hand carelessly across
the hilt of the Damascus blade, exposing,
almost to the shoulder, the rounded muscles
of the powerful arm of—a shepherd lad.

The caravan drew nearer and finally
halted when the leader was less than ten
paces from the white camel.

His envious eyes had been gloating over

the tempting prize as he approached; but gradually they became fastened upon that hand and arm, while the fingers that were playing gently upon the polished hilt seemed to beckon him on to test the gleaming blade beneath.

He could not see the beardless face, protected by the mantle. How could he know that that hand had never drawn a sword?

The whole appearance indicated a man without one thought of fear, and the savage chief realized that, before the white camel became his prize, some one beside its present owner would doubtless pay a dear price for it.

He was still determined to possess it, but the silent figure demanded and received respect from him.

Instead of the defiant words which were upon his tongue, he pronounced the desert greeting.

Kanana returned the salutation, and immediately asked, "Did the dust from Kah-

led's host blow over you when your foot
was on the sand of Bashra?''

The sheik drew back a little. It was a
slight but very suggestive motion, speaking
volumes to the keen eye of the Bedouin
boy. He had been leaning forward before,
more than is natural even to one tired out
with sitting upon a camel's back. It was
as if in his eagerness he was reaching forward to grasp the prize. Now he seemed
suddenly to have lost that eagerness.

Quickly, Kanana took advantage of the
hint. He drew from his bosom the letter
of the caliph, sealed with the great seal of
Mohammed, which every Mussulman could
recognize, and calmly holding it plainly in
view, he continued:

''The beak of the vulture has whitened,
instead of the bones he would have plucked.
The tooth of the jackal is broken, and not
the flesh he would have torn. Raschid
Airikat is neither at Damascus nor Mecca.
To-morrow morning he will be at Tayf.
He would have you meet him there. Say

to him, 'The fool hath eaten his own folly. The veiled messenger of the Prophet, sitting upon the sacred camel, glides with the night wind into the rising sun; for the fire is lighted in Hejaz that at Bashra shall cause the camels' necks to shine.' "

A decided change came over the savage face of the Arab sheik. He sat in silence for a moment, then, without a word, drove the prod into his camel.

There was a grunt and a gurgling wail, and the tired animal was moving on, followed by all the rest.

Kanana and his camel-driver were left alone. When they were well out of hearing the driver prostrated himself before Kanana, touching his forehead to the ground, and asked:

"Master, who was that sheik, with all his warriors, and who art thou that they should cower before thy word?"

"I am no one to receive your homage. Stand upon your feet!" almost shouted

Kanana. "I never saw nor heard of them until to-day."

He breathed a deep, quivering sigh, and leaned heavily upon the saddle; for every muscle in his body shook and trembled as the result of what had seemed so calm and defiant. He tried to replace the letter in his bosom, but his hand trembled so that he was obliged to wait.

"Thou knewest that he was of the tribe of Raschid Airikat, and that he came from Bashra," said the driver.

"I knew nothing," replied Kanana, petulantly, in the intense reaction. "How long have you been a man, well taught in killing other men, not to see what any cowardly shepherd boy could read? Were not their lances made of the same peculiar wood; and their camel saddles, were they not the same, stained with the deep dye of Bashra? Who should come out of the rising sun, with his camel licking the desert sand, if he came not from Bashra? Who should be going toward Mecca at this season, without a bur-

dened camel in his caravan, if he went not
to meet his chief for war? Why did Airikat crowd his caravan, day and night, if
he expected no one?"

"But, master, Airikat is at Mecca, not
at Tayf," said the camel-driver.

"Bedouin, where are your eyes and
ears?" exclaimed Kanana, scornfully.
"Your paltry beggars at the caliph's gate
carried my message swiftly. We had not
left the gate of Mecca out of sight when on
the road behind us came Airikat and four
followers. While you were struggling to
reach the white camel, they did their best
to overtake us both, but we outstripped
them. We kept upon the way till we had
passed the nightly caravan. They would
have to rest their horses at the well, and
the caravan would halt there, too. They
would inquire for us, and the caravan would
answer, 'We passed the white camel running like the wind toward Tayf.' Enough.
Airikat with his horsemen cannot reach
there before the next sunrise, and when he

learns the truth he will be five days behind us. From him and yonder caravan
by the help of Allah we are safe. If you
would learn a lesson, by the way, let it be
this: that man can conquer man without a
sword or lance. Sleep on it."

Setting the example, Kanana removed
the camel's saddle, fastened his hind foot
to his haunch with the twisted rope so that
he could not rise, and sank upon the sand
beside him, laying his head upon the creature's neck.

The last words which he heard from his
driver were: "Master, thou art mightier
than Airikat and all his warriors."

The sun beat fiercely down all day upon
his resting-place; but Kanana's sleep was
sweeter than if the cool starlight had been
over him, or a black tent of the Beni Sads;
because, for that one day at least, his head
was pillowed upon the white camel's neck.

It was late in the afternoon before he
woke, and the sun was setting when the little caravan was again prepared to start.

They were ready to mount when the driver came to the white camel. He laid his hand upon the dingy haunch, and said, in a voice that was strangely pleading for a fierce Bedouin:

"Master, do not crowd him over-hard to-night. He obeys too willingly. He is tired from a long journey. It is four weeks since he has rested. I would rather you would kill me than the white camel."

Kanana thought for a moment, then taking his shepherd's staff from the saddle, he replied:

"You can tell better than I how he should be driven. Mount him, and I will ride the dromedary."

To the driver this was only Arab sarcasm, and he hesitated till Kanana silently pointed his staff toward the saddle, and the driver was more afraid to refuse than to obey.

Kanana turned and mounted the dromedary.

As the camel rose to his feet, a strange

temptation sent the blood tingling to the driver's finger-tips.

The dromedary was unarmed. The messenger of Omar held only a shepherd's staff. Almost unconsciously his hand clutched the hilt of the Damascus blade, betraying the fact that it was better used to holding such a thing than the rope that led the white camel through Mecca.

Quickly the driver looked back, to see Kanana quietly watching him. Instantly his hand dropped the hilt, but it was too late. Scornfully Kanana said:

"Lo! every child of Ishmael, from the devout Raschid to the faithful camel-driver, will serve himself. Nay, keep the hand upon the sword. Perchance there will be better cause to use it than in defying me. From here our paths must separate. I promised that to-night I would lay out your course for you. It is northward, without swerving, for ten nights, at least."

"And whither goest thou, my master?"

"That only Allah can direct, from day to day. *La Illaha il Allah!*"

"And what is my mission to be?" asked the driver, anxiously.

"It is to seek the Beni Sads; to find the aged chief, the Terror of the Desert; to say to him, 'Kanana hath fulfilled his vow.' He hath not lifted the lance against Airi-kat; but thy white camel is returned to thee, bearing thy first-born upon his back. Go, and God go with thee!"

"Who art thou?" cried the man upon the white camel, starting from his seat as the dromedary gave the usual grunt, in answer to the prod, and moved away.

The Bedouin boy turned in the saddle, tore off the *abbe* and the mantle that covered him, and clad in the sheepskin coat and desert turban answered:

"I am thy brother Kanana, the coward of the Beni Sads!"

IX

FOR ALLAH AND ARABIA

"**K**ANANA! our Kanana!" cried the brother, striking the camel's neck. The dingy dignity of the great white camel was ruffled by the blow received, and he expressed his disapproval in a series of grunts before he made any attempt to start.

"Kanana! Kanana!" the brother called again, seeing the dromedary already merging into the shadows; but the only response he received was from the shepherd's staff, extended at arm's length pointing northward.

"My young brother shall not leave me in this way. He has no weapon of defense and only a little of the grain."

Again he struck the camel a sharp blow as the animal began very slowly to move forward. The black dromedary was hardly

100

distinguishable from the night, and was rapidly sinking into the deepening shadows before the camel was fairly on the way.

"Go!" cried the rider savagely, striking him again, and the camel moved a little faster; but he made slow and lumbering work, for he was not at all pleased with his treatment.

The rider's eyes were fixed intently upon the dim outline sinking away from him. The last he saw of it was the hand and arm, still holding the extended shepherd's staff, pointing to the north. Then all was lost.

He kept on in that direction for an hour, but it was evident that he had begun in the wrong way with the camel, and that he was not forcing him to anything like his speed of the night before.

It was beyond his power to overtake the dromedary, and doubly chagrined he gave up the race and turned northward.

The path before Kanana was the highway between Persia and Mecca. At some seasons it was almost hourly traversed, but

at midsummer only absolute necessity
drove the Arabs across the very heart of
the desert.

In the height of the rainy season there
were even occasional pools of water in the
hollows, here and there. Later there was
coarse, tough grass growing, sometimes for
miles along the way.

Little by little, however, they disappeared. Then the green of each oasis
shrank toward the center, about the spring
or well, and often before midsummer was
over, they too had dried away.

The prospect of loneliness, however, was
not at all disheartening to Kanana. He
had no desire to meet with any one, least
of all with such parties as would be apt
to cross the desert at this season.

If a moving shadow appeared in the distance, he turned well to one side and had
the dromedary lie down upon the sand till
it passed.

The black dromedary was fresh, and the
Bedouin boy knew well how to make the

most of his strength while it lasted; but it was for Allah and Arabia that they crossed the desert, and Kanana felt that neither his own life nor that of the dromedary could be accounted of value compared with the demand for haste.

He paid no heed to the usual camping-grounds for caravans, except to be sure that he passed two of them every night till the dromedary's strength began to fail.

Each morning the sun was well upon its way before he halted for the day, and long before it set again he was following his shadow upon the sand.

More and more the dromedary felt the strain. When twelve nights had passed, the pride of the caliph was anything but a tempting prize, and Kanana would hardly have troubled himself to turn out for a caravan even if he had thought it a band of robbers.

The Bedouin boy, too, was thoroughly worn and exhausted. For days they had been without water, checking their thirst

by chewing the prickly leaves of the little
desert vine that is the last sign of life upon
the drying sand. No dew fell at this season, and Kanana realized that it was only
a matter of hours as to how much longer
they could hold out.

Morning came without a sign of water
or of life, as far as the eye could reach.

The sun rose higher, and Kanana longed
for the sight of a human being as intensely
as at first he had dreaded it.

Nothing but the ghastly bones of men
and animals bleaching among the sand-
shrubs showed him that he was still upon
the highway to Bashra.

Out of the glaring silver-gray, the fiery
sun sailed into the lusterless blue of the
dry, hot sky, leaving the two separated by
the eternal belt of leaden clouds that never
rise above a desert-horizon and never dis-
perse in rain.

Kanana halted only for his morning
prayer, and, when it was finished, the petition that he added for himself was simply

"Water! water! O Allah! give us water."

Each day the heat had become more intense, and to-day it seemed almost to burn the very sand. As Kanana mounted again and started on, his tired eyes sought anxiously the glaring billows for some sign of life; but not a living thing, no shadow even, broke the fearful monotony.

There were gorgeous promises, but they did not deceive the eyes that had looked so often along the sand. There were great cities rising upon the distant horizon, with stately domes and graceful minarets such as were never known throughout the length and breadth of Arabia. And when the bells ceased tolling in Kanana's ears, he could hear the muezzin's call to prayer. Then the bells would toll again and he would mutter, "Water! water! O Allah! give us water."

He had no longer any heart to urge the tired dromedary to a faster pace. He knew that it would only be to see him fall, the sooner, upon the sand. The tired creature's head hung down till his nose touched the earth as he plodded slowly onward.

The sun rose higher. It was past the hour when they always stopped, but neither thought of stopping. Waiting would not bring the water to them, and the Bedouin boy knew well that to lie on the desert sand that day meant to lie there forever.

The dromedary knew it as well as his master, and without a word to urge him, he kept his feet slowly moving onward, like an automaton, with his nose thrust forward just above the sand, as though he too were pleading: "Water! water! O Allah! give us water."

His eyes were closed. His feet dragged along the sand. Kanana did not attempt to guide him, though he swayed from side to side, sometimes reeling and almost falling over low hillocks which he made no effort to avoid.

Kanana could scarcely keep his own eyes open. The glare of the desert was blinding; but their last hope lay in his watchfulness.

He struggled hard to keep back the treacherous drowsiness, but his head would drop upon one shoulder, then upon the other. He could have fallen from the saddle and stretched himself upon the sand to die without a struggle, had it not been for the caliph's letter in his bosom. Again and again he pressed his hand upon it to rouse himself, and muttered, "By the help of Allah, I will deliver it."

Each time that this roused him he shaded his eyes and sought again the sand before him; but glaring and gray it stretched away to the horizon, without one shadow save that of the forest of low and brittle sand-shrubs.

The burning sky grew black above him, and the desert became a fiery red. The dromedary did not seem like a living thing. He thought he was sitting upon his perch in the harvest field. The sun seemed cold, as its rays beat upon his head. He shiv-

ered and unconsciously drew the wings of
his turban over his face. No wonder it
was cold. It was the early morning under
Mount Hor. Yes, there were all the blue
forget-me-nots. How the stream rippled
and gurgled among them!

He started. What was that shock that
roused him? Was it the robbers coming
down upon him? He shook himself
fiercely. Was he sleeping? He struggled
to spring to his feet, but they were tangled
in something.

At last his blood-shot eyes slowly opened
and consciousness returned. The dromedary had fallen to the ground, beside—an
empty well.

Kanana struggled to his feet and looked
down among the rocks. The bottom was
as dry as the sand upon which he was
standing.

He looked back at the dromedary. Its
eyes were shut. Its neck was stretched
straight out before it on the sand, its head
rested upon the rocks of the well.

"Thou hast given thy life for Allah and Arabia," Kanana said, "and when the Prophet returns in his glory, he will remember thee."

He took the sack of camel's food from the saddle and emptied the whole of it where the dromedary could reach it. Then he cut the saddle-straps and dragged the saddle to one side. It was all that he could do for the dumb beast that had served him.

Suddenly he noticed that the sun was setting. All the long day he must have slept, while the poor dromedary had crept onward toward the well. It had not been a healthful sleep, but it refreshed him, and combined with the excitement of waking and working for the dromedary, he found his tongue less parched than before. Quickly he took a handful of wheat and began to chew it vigorously; a secret which has saved the life of many a Bedouin upon the great sea of sand.

For a moment he leaned upon the empty

saddle chewing the wheat, watching the sun sink into the sand and thinking.

"Thirteen days" he muttered. "I said fourteen when I started, but we have done better than three days in two. If we did not turn from the way to-day, this well is but one night from Bashra. *O Allah! Mahamoud rousol il Allah!* give thy servant life for this one night."

The dromedary had not moved to touch the food beside him, and there was no hope of further help from the faithful animal. Kanana stood beside it for a moment, laid his hand gratefully upon the motionless head, then took up his shepherd's staff and started on.

Sometimes waking, sometimes sleeping as he walked, sometimes thinking himself far away from the sands of Bashra, sometimes urging himself on with a realization that he must be near his journey's end, he pressed steadily on and on, hour after hour.

Sometimes he felt fresh enough to start

and run. Sometimes he wondered if he had the strength to lift his foot and put it forward another time. Sometimes he felt sure that he was moving faster than a caravan, and that he should reach Bashra before morning. Sometimes it seemed as though the willing spirit must leave the lagging flesh behind as he had left the dromedary, and go on alone to Bashra.

Then he would press the sacred letter hard against his bosom and repeat, "By the help of Allah I will deliver it!" And all the time, though he did not realize it, he was moving forward with swift and steady strides, almost as though he were inspired with superhuman strength.

Far away to the east a little spark of light appeared. It grew and rose, till above the clouds there hung a thin white crescent; the narrowest line of moonlight.

Kanana gave a cry of joy, for it was an omen which no Arab could fail to understand.

Then the air grew cold. The darkest

hour before the dawn approached, and the narrow moon served only to make the earth invisible.

The dread of meeting any one had long ago left Kanana's mind. First he had feared it. Then he had longed for it. Now he was totally indifferent. He looked at the sky above him to keep his course. He looked at the sand beneath his feet; but he did not once search the desert before him.

Suddenly he was roused from his lethargy. There were shadows just ahead. He paused, shaded his eyes from the sky and looked forward, long and earnestly.

"It is not sand-shrubs," he muttered. "It is too high. It is not Bashra. It is too low. It is not a caravan. It does not move. It has no beginning and no end," he added, as he looked to right and left.

"It is tents," he said a moment later, and a frown of anxiety gathered over his forehead. "Have I missed the way? No tribe so large as that would be tented near

Bashra. If I turn back I shall die. If I go on—*La Illaha il Allah!*" he murmured, and resolutely advanced.

As he drew nearer, the indistinguishable noises of the night in a vast encampment became plainly audible, but he did not hesitate.

Following the Arab custom for every stranger in approaching a Bedouin camp, he paused at the first tent he reached, and standing before the open front repeated the Mussulman salutation.

Some one within roused quickly, and out of the darkness a deep voice sounded in reply.

Then Kanana repeated:

"I am a wanderer upon the desert. I am far from my people." And the voice replied:

"If you can lift the lance for Allah and Arabia, you are welcome in the camp of Kahled the Invincible."

"*La Illaha il Allah!*" cried Kanana. "Guide me quickly to the tent of Kahled.

I am a messenger to him from the great Caliph Omar.''

The earth reeled beneath the feet of Kanana as the soldier led the way.

The general was roused without the formality of modern military tactics or even Mohammedan courtesies. A torch was quickly lighted. Kanana prostrated himself; then rising, he handed the precious packet to the greatest general who ever led the hosts of Mohammed.

Kahled the Invincible broke the seal, but before he had read a single word, the Bedouin boy fell unconscious upon the carpet of the tent.

As the soldiers lifted him, Kanana roused for an instant and murmured:

''By the dry well, one night to the southwest, my black dromedary is dying of thirst. In Allah's name, send him water! He brought the message from Mecca in thirteen days!'' Then the torch-light faded before his eyes, and Kanana's lips were sealed in unconsciousness.

X

A VAST Mohammedan army, with its almost innumerable followers, was marching towards Syria, to meet the hosts of the Emperor Heraclius.

Like a pillar of cloud the dust rose above the mighty throng.

Armed horsemen, ten thousand strong, rode in advance.

A veteran guard of scarred and savage men came next, mounted upon huge camels, surrounding Kahled the Invincible and his chief officers, who rode upon the strongest and most beautiful of Persian horses.

A little distance behind were thousands of fierce warriors mounted on camels and dromedaries. Then came another vast detachment of camels bearing the tents, furniture, and provisions of the army; these were followed by a motley throng, comprising the families of many of the tribes represented in the front, while still another powerful guard brought up the rear.

Behind the body-guard of Kahled and before the war-camels rode a smaller guard, in the center of which were two camels, bearing a litter between them.

Upon this litter lay Kanana, shielded from the sun by a goat's-hair awning; for almost of necessity the army moved by daylight. It started an hour after sunrise, resting two hours at noon, and halting an hour before sunset. It moved more rapidly than a caravan, however, and averaged twenty-five miles a day.

Close behind Kanana's litter walked a riderless dromedary. At the start it was haggard and worn. Its dark hair was burned to a dingy brown by the fierce heat of the desert; but even Kahled received less careful attention, and every day it gathered strength and held its head a little higher.

The black dromedary was not allowed to carry any burden, but was literally covered with gay-colored cloths; decorating the pride of Omar the Great, that had brought the good news from Mecca to Bashra in less than thirteen days.

Nothing pleasanter could have been announced to that terrible army of veterans surrounding the valiant Kahled, than that it was to face the mightiest host which the Emperor Heraclius could gather in all the north.

There was not one in all that throng who doubted, for an instant, that Kahled could conquer the whole world if he chose, in the name of Allah and the Prophet.

Many of the soldiers had followed him since the day, years before, when he made his first grand plunge into Persia. They had seen him made the supreme dictator of Babylonia. They had seen him send that remarkable message to the great monarch of Persia:

"Profess the faith of Allah and his

Prophet, or pay tribute to their servants.
If you refuse I will come upon you with a
host that loves death as much as you love
life.''

Once before had they seen him summoned from his triumphs in Persia, because all of the Mohammedan generals and
soldiers in Syria were not able to cope with
the power of Heraclius. They had seen
him invested with the supreme power by
the Caliph Abu-Bekr, Omar's predeces-
sor, and watched while, single-handed, he
fought and conquered the great warrior,
Romanus.

Most of them had been with him before
the walls of Damascus, when he besieged
that magnificently fortified city upon one
side, and fought and conquered an army of
a hundred thousand men upon the other
side, sent from Antioch, by Heraclius, for
the relief of the great city. Then they wit-
nessed the fall of Damascus, and followed
Kahled as he attacked and put to flight an
army outnumbering his by two to one, and

equipped and drilled in the most modern
methods of Roman warfare.

They had fought with him in the fiercest
battles ever recorded of those desert lands,
and they only knew him as Kahled the Invincible.

After Abu-Bekr had died and Omar the
Great had taken his place, the proud soldiers saw their general unjustly deposed
and given such minor work as tenting about
the besieged cities, while others did the
fighting, until he left Syria in disgust.

No wonder they were glad to see him recalled to take his proper place. They
jested without end about the cowards who
were frightened because Heraclius had
threatened to annihilate the Mussulmans.
And the march was one grand holiday, in
spite of heat and hardships.

As Kanana lay in his litter and listened
to these bursts of eloquence in praise of
the general, he was often stirred with ar-
dent patriotism and almost persuaded to
cast his lot among the soldiers; but the

same odd theories which before had prevented his taking up a lance, restrained
him still.

On the fourth day he left the litter and
took his seat upon the black dromedary.
Kahled directed that costly garments and
a sword and lance be furnished him, but
Kanana prostrated himself before the general and pleaded: "My father, I never
held a lance, and Allah knows me best in
this sheepskin coat."

Kahled frowned, but Kanana sat upon
the decorated dromedary precisely as he
left the perch in the harvest-field. He expected to take his place with the camp-followers in the rear, but found that he was
still to ride in state surrounded by the veteran guard. Indeed, he became a figure so
celebrated and conspicuous that many a
warrior in passing, after prostrating himself before the general, touched his forehead to the ground before Kanana and the
black dromedary.

It might have made a pleasant dream, while sitting upon the perch in the harvest-field, but the reality disturbed him, and again he began to plan some means of escape.

He carefully computed the position of the Beni Sad encampment, and determined the day when the army would pass but a few miles to the east of it.

One who has not lived upon the desert, and seen it illustrated again and again, can scarcely credit the accuracy with which a wandering Bedouin can locate the direction and distance to any point with which he is familiar; but even then Kanana was at a loss as to how to accomplish his purpose when the whole matter was arranged for him, and he was supplied with a work which he could perform for Allah and Arabia, still holding his shepherd's staff and wearing his sheepskin coat.

The army halted for the night upon the eve of the day when it would pass near the

encampment of the Beni Sads. The tent
which Kanana occupied was pitched next
that of Kahled.

He sat upon the ground eating his sup-
per. All about him was the clatter and
commotion of the mighty host preparing
for the night, when he heard an officer reporting to the general that in three days
the supply of grain would be exhausted.

"My father," he exclaimed, prostrating
himself before the general, "thy servant's
people, the Beni Sads, must be less than a
night's journey to the north and west.
They were harvesting six weeks ago, and
must have five hundred camel-loads of
grain to sell. Bid me go to them to-night,
and, with the help of Allah, by the sunrise
after to-morrow it shall be delivered to thy
hand."

Kahled had formed a very good opinion
of the Bedouin boy. He had noticed his
uneasiness, and, suspecting that he would
make an endeavor to escape, he had been
searching for some occupation that should

prevent it by rendering him more content to remain. He felt that a time might come when Kanana, with his sheepskin coat and shepherd's staff, might be of greater value to him than many a veteran with costly *abbe* and gleaming sword.

The result was an order that, one hour after sunset, Kanana should start, at the head of a hundred horsemen, with ten camels laden with treasure for the purchase of grain, with twenty camels bearing grain-sacks, and one with gifts from Kahled to the Terror of the Desert, in acknowledgment of the service rendered by his son.

When he had purchased what grain the Beni Sads would sell, he was to continue in advance of the army, securing supplies to the very border of Syria.

Kanana was no prodigy of meekness that he should not appreciate this distinction. A prouder boy has never lived, in Occident or Orient, than the Bedouin shepherd who sat upon the black dromedary

and publicly received the general's blessing and command of the caravan.

In any other land there might have been
rebellion among a hundred veteran horsemen, when placed under command of a boy
in a sheepskin coat, armed only with a shepherd's staff, but there was no man of them
who had not heard wonderful tales of Kanana's courage; and the shepherd who had
left the harvest field six weeks before,
known only as the coward of the Beni Sads,
set his face toward home that night, followed by a hundred savage warriors who
obeyed him as one of the bravest of all the
Bedouins.

As the caravan moved rapidly over the
plain, bearing its costly burden, it is hardly
surprising that the beardless chief recalled
his last interview with his angry father,
when that veteran sheik refused to trust
him with a single horse to start upon his
mission; but he was none the less anxious
to reach his father's tent and receive his
father's blessing.

XI

THE SACRED GIRDLE

SHORTLY after midnight five horsemen who rode in advance returned to report a large encampment, far away upon the left. Then Kanana took the lead as a brave Bedouin chieftain should, and, followed by the caravan, approached the smoldering fires which betrayed the location of the camp.

He rode directly toward the tent of the sheik, which always stands in the outer line, farthest from a river or upon the side from which the guests of the tribe will be most likely to approach.

As he approached, a shadow rose silently out of the shadows. It sniffed the air. Then there was a faint grunt of satisfaction and the shadow sank down into the shadows again.

Kanana slipped from the back of the

dromedary without waiting for him to lie down, and, running forward to the white camel, whispered, "I knew that thou wouldst know me."

The Terror of the Desert appeared at the tent door with a hand raised in blessing.

Kanana ran to his father with a cry of joy, and the white-haired sheik threw his arms about the neck of his son and kissed him, saying:

"Forgive me, Kanana, my brave Kanana! I said that thou hadst come to curse me with thy cowardice, and lo! thou hast done grander, braver deeds than I in all my years! Verily, thou hast put me to shame, but it is with courage, not with cowardice."

Kanana tried to speak, but tears choked him. All alone he could calmly face a score of savage robbers, armed to the teeth, but suddenly he discovered that he was only a boy, after all. He had almost forgotten it. And in helpless silence he clung to his father's neck.

The old sheik roused himself.

"Kanana," he exclaimed, "why am I silent? The whole tribe waits to welcome thee. Ho! every one who sleepeth!" he called aloud, "awake! awake! Kanana is returned to us!"

Far and near the cry was repeated, and a moment later the people came hurrying to greet the hero of the Beni Sads.

Not only had the brother returned with the white camel and a glowing account of his rescue by the veiled messenger of the caliph, but a special officer had come, by a passing caravan, bearing to the Terror of the Desert a bag of gold and the congratulations of Omar the Great, that he was the father of such a son.

Now the gifts from Kahled the Invincible arrived, and the hundred horsemen obeying the voice of Kanana. The Beni Sads could scarcely believe their eyes and ears.

Torches were lighted. Fires were rekindled and, before sunrise, the grandest of all grand Bedouin feasts was in full glory.

Vainly, however, did the old sheik bring out the best robe to put it on him; with a ring for his hand and shoes for his feet; in a custom for celebrating a son's return which was old when the story of the Prodigal was told.

Kanana only shook his head and answered, "My father, Allah knows me best barefooted and in this sheepskin coat."

The Bedouin seldom tastes of meat except upon the occasion of some feast.

When a common guest arrives, unleavened bread is baked and served with *ayesh,* a paste of sour camel's milk and flour. But Kanana was not a common guest.

For one of higher rank coffee and melted butter is prepared, but these were not enough for a welcome to Kanana.

For one still higher a kid or lamb is boiled in camel's milk and placed in a great wooden dish covered with melted fat and

surrounded by a paste of wheat that has
been boiled and dried and ground and
boiled again with butter.

Twenty lambs and kids were thus prepared, but the people were not satisfied.
Nothing was left but the greatest and
grandest dish which a Bedouin tribe can
add to a feast in an endeavor to do honor
to its noblest guest. Two she-camels were
killed and the meat quickly distributed to
be boiled and roasted. All for the boy
who had left them, six weeks before, with
no word of farewell but the parting taunt
of a rat-catcher.

While the men were eating the meat and
drinking camel's milk and coffee, the
women sang patriotic songs, often substi-
tuting Kanana's name for that of some
great hero; and when the men had finished
and the women gathered in the maharems
to feast upon what was left, the Terror of
the Desert, roused to the highest pitch of
patriotism, declared his intention to join
the army of Kahled, and nearly two hun-

dred of the Beni Sads resolved to follow
him.

It was nearly noon when Kanana and
those who were with him went to sleep in
the goat's-hair tents, leaving the whole
tribe at work, packing the grain-sacks,
loading the camels, and cleaning their
weapons for war.

Kanana performed his mission faith-
fully, little dreaming that Kahled's one de-
sign in placing it in his hands was to keep
him with the army for services of much
greater importance.

The time which the general anticipated
came when the hosts of Kahled, joined by
the Mohammedan armies of Syria and
Arabia, were finally encamped at Yermonk
upon the borders of Palestine.

Kanana was summoned to the general's
tent and, trembling like the veriest coward
in all the world, he fell upon his face before the man to whom was entrusted the
almost hopeless task of rescuing Arabia.

To Kahled alone all eyes were turned and
Kanana trembled, not because he was
frightened, but because he was alone in the
tent with one who seemed to him but little
less than God himself.

Kahled's words were always few and
quickly spoken.

"Son of the Terror of the Desert," said
he, "many conflicting rumors reach me
concerning the approaching enemy. I
want the truth. I want it quickly. What
dost thou require to aid thee in performing this duty?"

Kanana's forehead still touched the
ground. Overwhelmed by this sudden
order, an attempt to obey which, meant
death, without mercy, without one chance
in a hundred of escape, he altogether forgot to rise.

Kahled sat in silence, understanding human nature too well to disturb the boy, and
for five minutes neither moved. Then Kanana rose slowly and his voice trembled a

little as he replied, "My father, I would have thy fleetest horse, thy blessing, and thy girdle."

Kahled the Invincible wore a girdle that was known to every soldier and camp-follower of the army. It was of camel's-skin, soft-tanned and colored with a brilliant Persian dye, which as far away as it could be seen at all, no one could mistake.

It was part of a magnificent curtain which once hung in the royal palace of Babylon. It pleased the fancy of the fierce warrior, and he wore it as a girdle till it became his only insignia. There was not a color like it within hundreds of miles at least, and when the people saw it they knew that it was Kahled.

"Take what horse thou wilt," replied the general. "I give thee, now, my blessing." Then he hesitated for a moment. Had Kanana asked a hundred camels or a thousand horsemen he would have added, "Take them." As it was, he said, a little doubtfully, "What wouldst thou with my girdle?"

In all the direct simplicity which clung to him in spite of everything, Kanana replied: "I would hide it under my coat; I would that it be proclaimed throughout the army that some one has fled to the enemy with the sacred girdle, and that a great reward be offered to him who shall return to Kahled any fragment of it he may find."

Without another word, the general unwound the sacred girdle, and Kanana, reverently touching it to his forehead, bound it about him under his sheepskin coat.

Kneeling, he received the blessing, and leaving the tent, he selected the best of Kahled's horses and disappeared in the darkness, alone.

The next morning an oppressive sense of inaction hung about the headquarters.

The only order issued accompanied an announcement of the loss of the sacred girdle.

Every soldier was commanded to be on the watch for it, to seize and to return at once to Kahled, even the smallest fragment which might be found.   For this the fortunate man was promised as many gold coins as, lying flat, could be made to touch the piece which he returned.

XII

KANANA'S MESSENGERS

FAR and wide the impatient soldiers asked, "Why is the army inactive?"

"Is not the motto of Kahled 'Waiting does not win'?"

"Has he not taught us that action is the soul and secret of success?"

"Does he not realize that the hosts of Heraclius are bearing down upon us, that he leaves us sitting idly in our tents?"

"Is Kahled the Invincible afraid?"

Such were the questions which they put to their officers, but no one dared carry them to the general, who sat in his tent without speaking, from sunrise to sunset, the first day after the girdle disappeared.

"Is it the loss of his girdle?"

"Did he not conquer Babylonia without it?"

135

"Does he not fight in the name of Allah and the Prophet? Could a bright-colored girdle give him strength?"

Thus the second day went by.

Kahled the Invincible was silent and sullen, and the impression grew and grew that in some way the safety and success of the whole army depended upon the recovery of that girdle.

So intense was this sentiment, that when at midnight, after the third day, it was reported that a fragment of the girdle had been captured by some scouts, and was then being taken to the general's tent, the whole army roused itself and prepared for action.

Not an order had been issued, yet every soldier felt instinctively that the coming morning would find him on the march.

It was midnight. For a day Kahled had not even tasted food. He sat alone in his tent upon a Persian ottoman. A bronze vessel from Babylonia, filled with oil, stood near the center of the tent. Fragments of burning wick, floating in the oil, filled the tent with a mellow, amber light.

There was excitement without, but Kahled did not heed it till a soldier unceremoniously entered, bearing in his hand a part of the curtain from the palace of Babylon.

With a sudden ejaculation Kahled caught it from the soldier's hand, but ashamed of having betrayed an emotion, he threw it carelessly upon the rug at his feet, handing the soldier a bag of gold, and bidding him see how many pieces, lying flat, could touch it.

The soldier worked slowly, carefully planning the position as he laid the pieces down, and Kahled watched him as indifferently as though he were only moving men upon the Arab's favorite checkerboard.

When every piece that could was touching the camel skin, the soldier returned the bag, half-emptied, and began to gather up his share.

Kahled deliberately emptied the bag, bidding him take the whole and go.

He was leaving the tent when the general called him back. He had picked up the skin, and was carelessly turning it over in his hand. It was neatly cut from the girdle, in the shape of a shield, a little over a foot in width.

"How did you come by it?" Kahled asked indifferently.

"We were searching the plain, a day's journey to the north," the soldier answered. "We were looking for travelers who might bring tidings of the enemy. We saw four strangers, Syrians, riding slowly, and a shepherd who seemed to be their guide. Upon his horse's front, hung like a breastplate, where every eye could see, was yonder piece of the sacred girdle. We dashed upon them, and the cowards ran. The shepherd was the last to turn. I was ahead, but not near enough to reach him, so I threw my lance. He fell from his horse and—"

"You killed him?" shrieked the general, springing to his feet and dropping the camel skin.

"No! no!" gasped the frightened soldier. "I only tried to. He wore a coat of sheepskin. It was too thick for my lance. He sprang to his feet, tore the lance from his coat, and ran after the rest, faster even than they could ride, leaving his horse behind."

"'Tis well," muttered the general, and he devoutly added, "Allah be praised for that sheepskin coat!"

The soldier left the tent, and going nearer to the light, Kahled examined the fragment of the sacred girdle. It was double. Two pieces had been cut and the edges joined together.

He carefully separated them, and upon the inner side found what he evidently expected.

These words had been scratched upon the leather, and traced with blood:

"Sixty thousand, from Antioch and

Aleppo, under Jababal the traitor, encamp two days from Yermonk, north, waiting for Manuel with eighty thousand Greeks and Syrians, now six days away. Still another army is yet behind. Thy servant goes in search of Manuel when this is sent.''

"Allah be praised for that sheepskin coat!'' Kahled repeated, placing the fragment in his belt, and walking slowly up and down the tent.

"Jababal is two days to the north,'' he added presently. "A day ago Manuel was six days behind him. He will be still three days behind when I reach Jababal, and while he is yet two days away, the sixty thousand in advance will be destroyed.''

An order was given for ten thousand horsemen and fifteen thousand camel riders to start for the north at once. The soldiers expected it, and were ready even before the general.

Four days and a night went by, and they were again encamped at Yermonk; but

Jababal's army of sixty thousand men, was a thing of the past.

Again a strip of the girdle was discovered. This time it hung upon the neck of a camel leading into the camp a long caravan laden with grain and fruit.

The camel-driver reported that one had met them while they were upon the way to supply the army of Manuel. He had warned them that Manuel would simply confiscate the whole and make them prisoners, and had promised that if they turned southward instead, to the camp of Kahled, with the talisman which he hung about the camel's neck, they should be well received and fairly treated.

From this talisman Kahled learned that the army of Manuel was almost destitute of provisions, and that a detachment with supplies was another five or six days behind.

The general smiled as he thought how the Bedouin boy had shrewdly deprived the hungry enemy of a hundred and fifty camel-

loads of food, while he secured for himself an excellent messenger to his friends.

During the night Manuel's magnificent
army arrived, and encamped just north of
the Mohammedans. Manuel chose for his
citadel a high cliff that rose abruptly out
of the plain between the two armies, and
ended in a precipitous ledge toward Arabia.

Standing upon the brow of this cliff, a
little distance from the tent of Manuel, one
could look far down the valley, over the
entire Mohammedan encampment.

When morning dawned, the prince sent
for the leading Mohammedan generals to
confer with him concerning terms of
peace. He offered to allow the entire army
to retire unmolested, if hostages were
given that the Arabs should never again
enter Syria.

The Mohammedan generals, who had
been thoroughly dismayed at the sight of
the Grecian phalanx, thanked Allah for
such a merciful deliverance, and instantly

voted to accept. The real authority, however, rested with Kahled, who replied,
"Remember Jababal!"

With so many in favor of peace, Manuel hoped for an acceptance of his terms,
and proposed that they consider the matter
for a day.

Kahled, with his hand upon the camel-
skin in his belt, replied again: "Remember Jababal!"

He realized that his only hope of victory
lay in striking a tired and hungry enemy,
and that each hour's delay was dangerous.
Less than half an hour later he was riding along the line of battle shouting the
battle cry:

"Paradise is before you! Fight for
it!"

The soldiers were ready, and there began the most desperate struggle that was
ever waged upon the plains of Syria.

All day long the furious conflict raged.
Three times the Bedouins were driven
back. Three times the cries and entreaties

of their women and children in the rear urged them to renew the fight, and again they plunged furiously upon the solid Grecian phalanx.

Night came, and neither army had gained or lost, but among the Bedouin captives taken by the Greeks were several who recognized Kanana. They saw him moving freely about the enemy's camp. They learned that he was supposed to be a servant who had fled, with other camp-followers, at the time of the slaughter of Jababal's army. They could see in it nothing but cowardly desertion. They said:

"He was afraid that we should be conquered, and instead of standing by us to fight for Arabia, he ran to the enemy to hide himself;" and in their anger they betrayed him. They reported to the Greeks that he was a Bedouin, of the army of Kahled, not a Syrian servant of Jababal.

Kanana was quickly seized, bound and dragged into the presence of the prince. Manuel had suspected that some one had betrayed both Jababal and himself to Kahled, and chagrined at the result of the first day's battle, he fiercely accused Kanana.

Calmly the Bedouin boy admitted that it was he who had given the information, and he waited without flinching as Manuel drew his sword.

"Boy, dost thou not fear to die?" he exclaimed, as he brandished his sword before Kanana.

"I fear nothing!" replied Kanana proudly.

"Take him away and guard him carefully," muttered the prince. "Dying is too easy for such as he. He must be tortured first."

The second day and the third were like the first. The army of the Prophet fought with a desperation that never has been equaled. The Ishmaelite counted his life as nothing so that he saw a Greek fall with him. It was the fate of Allah and Arabia for which they fought, and they stood as though rooted to the ground, knowing of no retreat but death.

Again and again their general's voice rang loud above the clashing arms:

"Paradise is before you if you fight! Hell waits for him who runs!" And they fought and fought and fought, and not a man dared turn his back.

Again and again the Grecian phalanx advanced, but they found a wall before them as solid as the cliff behind them.

When a Bedouin lay dead he ceased to fight, but not before; and the moment he fell, another sprang forward from behind to take his place.

XIII

THE LANCE OF KANANA

THE army of the Prophet had not retreated one foot from its original
position, when night brought the third
day's battle to a close.

Kahled sank upon the ground among his
soldiers, while the women from the rear
brought what refreshment they could to
the tired warriors.

All night he lay awake beside his gray
battle-horse, looking at the stars and thinking.

Flight or death would surely be the result of the coming day. Even Kahled the
Invincible, had given up all hope of victory.

He was too brave a man to fly, but he
was also too brave to force others to stand
and be slaughtered for his pride.

It was a bitter night for him, but as the

eastern sky was tinged with gray, he at last resolved to make the sacrifice himself, and save such of his people as he could.

The women and children, with the wounded who could be moved, must leave at once, taking all that they could carry with them, and scatter themselves in every direction.

When they were well away, he, with such as preferred to stand and die with him, would hold the foe in check while the rest of the army retreated, with orders to march at once to Mecca and Medina, and hold those two sacred cities as long as a man remained alive.

He breathed a deep sigh when the plan was completed, and rising, mounted his tired charger, to see that it was properly executed.

It was the first time in his career that Kahled the Invincible had ordered a retreat, and his only consolation was that he was neither to lead nor join in it.

In the camp of Manuel the same dread

of the coming day clouded every brow.
Food was entirely exhausted. Horses and
camels had been devoured. They had
neither the means with which to move
away, nor the strength to stand their
ground.

Their solid phalanx was only what the
enemy saw along the front. Rank after
rank had been supplied from the rear till
there was nothing left to call upon.

All that remained of the eighty thousand
iron-hearted fighters—the pride of the Emperor Heraclius—as they gathered about
the low camp fires, confessed that they
were overmatched by the sharper steel of
Mohammedan zeal and Bedouin patriotism.

Manuel and his officers knew that for at
least three days no relief could reach them;
they knew, too, that they could not endure
another day of fighting.

"If we could make them think that their
men are deserting and joining us, we might
frighten them," suggested an officer.

"Send for the spy," said Manuel quickly, "and let it be proclaimed to the other prisoners that all who will join us shall be set free, and that those who refuse shall be slaughtered without mercy."

Haggard and worn Kanana stood before him. For fifty hours he had lain bound, in a cave at the foot of the cliff, without a drop of water or a morsel of food.

"I am about to torture thee," said the prince. "Thou hast wronged me more than thy sufferings can atone, but I shall make them as bitter as I can. Hast thou anything to say before the work begins?"

Kanana thought for a moment, then, hesitating as though still doubtful, he replied:

"When the tempest rages on the desert, doth not the camel lay him down, and the young camel say to the drifting sand, 'Cover me; kill me, I am helpless'? But among the captives taken by the prince, I saw an old man pass my cave. He is full of years, and for him I would part my lips.

I hear that the prince will have the prisoners slain, but it is not the custom of my
people to make the women, the old men, and
the children suffer with the rest. May it
please the prince to double every torture
he has prepared for me, and in exchange
to set that old man free?"

"Who is he?" asked the prince.

"The one with a long white beard.
There are not two," replied Kanana.

"And what is he to you?"

Kanana hesitated.

"He shall die unless you tell me," said
the prince, and Kanana's cold lips trembled as he whispered:

"He is my father."

" 'Tis well," said Manuel. "Let him be
brought."

The old man entered, but paused at the
opposite side of the tent, looking reproachfully at his son. He had heard from the
other captives how they had discovered
Kanana, a deserter in the hour of danger,
living in the tents of the enemy. Even he

had believed the tale, and he was enough of a patriot to be glad that they betrayed his son.

"Is this thy father?" asked the prince. "He does not look it in his eyes."

Kanana simply bowed his head.

That look was piercing his heart far deeper than the threats of torture; but Manuel continued:

"You have offered to suffer every torture I can devise if I will set him free. But you have not compassed your debt to me. You gave to Kahled the information by which he conquered Jababal. You gave him information which prevented his making terms of peace with me. But for you I should be on my way to Mecca and Medina, to sweep them from the earth. But I like courage, and you have shown more of it than Kahled himself. It is a pity to throw a heart like yours under a clod of earth, and I will give you an opportunity to save both yourself and your father. Stand upon the brow of the cliff yonder, as the sun comes up. There, according to the custom of your people, wave this lance above your head. Shout your own name and your father's, so that all of your people can hear, and tell them that in one hour thirty thousand Arabs will draw the sword for the cause of Heraclius. Then throw the lance, and if your aim be good, and you do kill an Arab, that moment I will set thy father free, and thou shalt be made a prince among my people. Do not refuse me, or, after I have tortured thee, with red-hot irons I will burn out thy father's eyes, lest he should still look savagely upon thy corpse!"

He had scarcely ceased speaking when the old sheik exclaimed:

"My son! My Kanana, I have wronged thee! Forgive me if thou canst, but let him burn out my eyes! Oh! not for all the eyes that watch the stars would I have a son of mine a traitor. Thou wouldst not lift a lance before. I charge thee now, by Allah, lift it not for any price that can be offered thee by this dog of an infidel!'

Kanana did not look at his father. His eyes were fixed on Manuel, and when all was still, he asked:

"Will the prince allow his captive to sit alone till sunrise and consider his offer?"

"Take him out upon the cliff and let him sit alone," said Manuel; "but have the irons heated for his father's eyes."

Kanana chose a spot whence he could overlook the valley, and whatever his first intentions may have been, he changed them instantly, with his first glance. He started, strained his eyes, and looked as far as his keen sight could pierce the gray light of early morning.

Then his head sank lower and lower over his hands, lying in his lap, till the wings of his turban completely covered them. He did not move or look again.

In that one glance he had recognized the result of Kahled's last resolve. In the gray distance he saw that laden camels were moving to the south. He saw the dark spots, most distant in the valley, suddenly disappear. They were folding their tents! They were moving away! Kahled the Invincible had ordered a retreat.

Kanana knew that to retreat at that moment meant death to Arabia, but he did not move again till an officer touched him on the shoulder, and warned him that in a moment more the sun would rise.

With a startled shudder he rose and entered Manuel's tent.

"Is the word of the prince unchanged?" he asked. "If I speak the words and throw the lance and kill an Arab, that moment will he set my father free?"

"I swear it by all the powers of earth and heaven!" replied the prince.

"Give me the lance," said Kanana.

His father crouched against the tent, muttering: "For such an act, Kanana, when I am set free I will find first a fire with which to heat an iron, and burn my own eyes out."

Kanana did not heed him. He took the

lance, tested it, and threw it scornfully upon the ground.

"Give me a heavier one!" he exclaimed. "Do you think me like your Greek boys, made of wax? Give me a lance that, when it strikes, will kill."

They gave him a heavier lance.

"The hand-rest is too small for a Bedouin," he muttered, grasping it; "but wait! I can remedy that myself. Come. Let us have it over with."

As he spoke he tore a strip from beneath his coat, and, turning sharply about, walked before them to the brink of the cliff, winding the strip firmly about the hand-rest of the lance.

Upon the very edge he stood erect and waited.

The sun rose out of the plain, and flashed with blinding force upon the Bedouin boy, clad in his sheepskin coat and desert turban, precisely as it had found him in the porch of Aaron's tomb, upon the summit of Mount Hor.

His hand no longer held a shepherd's staff, but firmly grasped a Grecian lance, that gleamed and flashed as fiercely as the sun.

Upon Mount Hor he was bending forward, eagerly shading his eyes, anxiously looking away into the dim distance, searching the path of his destiny.

Now there was no eagerness. Calmly he stood there. Vainly the sun flashed in his clear, wide-open eyes. He did not even know that it was shining.

Not a muscle moved. Why was he waiting?

"Are you afraid?" muttered the prince, who had come as near as possible without being too plainly seen from below. "Remember your old father's eyes."

Kanana did not turn his head, but calmly answered:

"Do you see yonder a man upon a gray horse, moving slowly among the soldiers? He is coming nearer, nearer. That man is Kahled the Invincible. If he should come within range of the lance of Kanana, I suppose that Manuel would be well pleased to wait?"

"Good boy! Brave boy!" replied the prince. "When thou hast made thy mind to do a thing, thou doest it admirably. Kill him, and thou shalt be loaded down with gold till the day when thou diest of old age."

Kanana made no reply, but standing in bold relief upon the cliff, watched calmly and waited, till at last Kahled the Invincible left the line of soldiers, and alone rode nearer to the cliff.

"Now is your chance! Now! now!" exclaimed the prince.

Slowly Kanana raised the lance. Three times he waved it above his head. Three times he shouted:

"I am Kanana, son of the Terror of the Desert!" in the manner of the Bedouin who challenges an enemy to fight, or meets a foe upon the plain.

For a moment, then, he hesitated. The

next sentence was hard to speak. He knew too well what the result would be. It needed now no straining of the eyes to see his destiny.

All the vast army down below was look-ing up at him. Thousands would hear his words. Tens of thousands would see what followed them.

"Go on! go on!" the prince ejaculated fiercely.

Kanana drew a deep breath and shouted:
"In one hour thirty thousand Arabs will draw the sword in the army of Heraclius!"

Then gathering all his strength, he hurled the lance directly at the great Mo-hammedan general, who had not moved since he began to speak.

Throughout those two great armies one might have heard a sparrow chirp, as the gleaming, flashing blade fell like a meteor from the cliff.

The aim was accurate. The Bedouin boy cringed, and one might have imagined that it was even more accurate than he meant. It pierced the gray charger. The war-horse of Kahled plunged forward and fell dead upon the plain.

A fierce howl rose from the ranks of the Ishmaelites. Men and women shrieked and yelled.

"Kanana the traitor! A curse upon the traitor Kanana!" rent the very air.

Such was the confusion which followed that, had the Greeks been ready to advance, a thousand might have put a hundred thousand Bedouins to flight. But they were not ready.

Kanana stood motionless upon the cliff. He heard the yells of "Traitor!" but he knew that they would come, and did not heed them.

Calmly he watched till Kahled gained his feet, dragged the lance from his dying horse, and with it in his hand, hurried toward the soldiers.

Only once he turned, and for an instant looked up at the solitary figure upon the cliff. He lifted his empty hand, as though it were a blessing and not a malediction, he bestowed upon the Bedouin boy; then he disappeared.

With a deep, shivering sigh, Kanana pressed one hand beneath his sheepskin coat. A sharp contortion passed over him, but he turned about and stood calmly, face to face with Manuel.

"You did well," said the prince, "but you did not kill an Arab. It was for that I made my promise."

" 'And if you kill an Arab,' " gasped Kanana, " 'that moment I will set your father free'! Those were the prince's words! That was his promise, bound by all the powers of earth and heaven! He will keep it! He will not dare defy those powers, for I have killed an Arab!"

Clutching the sheepskin coat, Kanana tore it open, and, above a brilliant girdle, they saw a dagger buried in his bleeding breast. He tottered, reeled, stepped backward, and fell over the brink of the cliff.

"You may as well go free," said Manuel, turning to the sheik. "A monstrous sacrifice has just been made to purchase your liberty."

Turning abruptly he entered his tent to consider, with his officers, the next result.

"I think they are flying," an officer reported, coming from the cliff. "The horse-men and camels are hurrying into the hills. Only foot soldiers seem remaining in the front."

"Let every soldier face them who has strength to stand!" commanded the prince. "Put everything to the front, and if they fly give them every possible encouragement."

The order was obeyed, and the fourth day of battle began; but it was spiritless and slow.

The Bedouins, with their constantly thinning ranks, stood with grim determination where their feet rested, but they made no effort to advance.

The wearied out and starving Grecian phalanx simply held its ground. The

prince was not there to urge his soldiers
on. The voice of Kahled did not sound
among the Mussulmans.

An hour went by.

Suddenly there was an uproar in the rear
of the army of Heraclius. There was a
wild shout, a clash of arms, and the watch-
word of Islam rang above the tumult, in
every direction.

Ten thousand horse and twenty thousand war-camels poured in upon that de-
fenseless rear, and, even as Kanana had
declared, in just one hour there were thirty
thousand Arabs wielding their savage
swords in the army of Heraclius.

Another hour went by. The battle cry
of Kahled ceased. The shout of victory
rang from the throats of the Mussulmans.
Manuel and all his officers were slain. The
magnificent army of Heraclius was literally
obliterated.

Treasure without limit glutted the conquered camp. Arabia was saved.

Quickly the soldiers erected a gorgeous

throne and summoned Kahled to sit upon •
it, while they feasted about him and did him
honor as their victorious and invincible
leader.

The veteran warrior responded to their
call, but he came from his tent with his
head bowed down, bearing in his arms a
heavy burden. Slowly he mounted the
platform, and upon the sumptuous throne
he laid his burden down.

It was the bruised and lifeless body of
Kanana.

With trembling hand the grim chief drew
back the sheepskin coat, and all men then
beheld, bound about the Bedouin boy, the
sacred girdle!

"I gave it to him," said Kahled solemnly; "and upon the fragments you have
returned to me, he wrote the information by
which we conquered Jababal and Manuel.
You saw him throw this lance at me; you
called him 'traitor!' but about the hand-
rest there was wound this strip. See! In
blood—in his blood—these words are writ-

ten here: 'Do not retreat. The infidels
are starving and dying.   Strike them in the
rear.' It was his only means of reaching
me. It was not the act of a traitor. No!
It was the Lance of Kanana that rescued
Arabia."

THE END

THE LANCE OF KANANA

This is an exciting story about an Arabian lad who
has many adventures. As you read about his experi-
ences, you will learn a great deal about Arabia, the
Bedouins, and life on the desert. This index will help
you to locate any particular topic when you want to
refresh your memory on some feature of desert life.